32 MINUTES

By Matthew Wade

Published by New Generation Publishing in 2021

First Edition

ISBN

Paperback	978-1-80031-280-7
Hardback	978-1-80031-279-1
Ebook	978-1-80031-278-4

www.newgeneration-publishing.com

 New Generation Publishing

About the Author

Matthew Wade is a British sci-fi and supernatural author. He started out his creative career as a lead guitar player and has toured the country in the back of many old broken-down vans. Since then, he has turned his hand to his other passion – writing.

Matthew lives in London with his wife and children, loves loud music, books (of course) and has never met a coffee machine he hasn't liked.

From the Author

This last year has been incredibly tough for a lot of people. It will be a year that future generations will be taught about in schools, and we will be able to recount our own stories to those who ask us as witnesses of history.

I take comfort in the fact that one day this will all be a distant memory. It will be in the past, and we will come out the other side and be together again.

We will meet our friends and families, eat, drink, laugh and play.

We will reminisce and remember and try to forget.

We will all have our own experiences and take on what happened.

We will all have a very different tale to tell.

For me, the enforced stay at home gave me more time to be creative and spawned this novel, and I am fortunate that I have this as a tool to fall back on.

The process of writing is a therapeutic one for me, and something that allows me to escape into my own created worlds and lose track of time as I tell myself another story.

I hope this gives you some escape and distraction for a moment, as much as the writing of it did for me.

Thank you to my parents for giving me love, support, and teaching me self-belief, drive and how to shoot for the stars.

Thank you to my wife and children for grounding me.

Thank you to Jackie and Sarah for reading first.

Thank you to David, Saskia, Rachel and all of the guys at New Generation Publishing for supporting me.

And once again thank you, dear reader, for being here.

As a great man once told me: "Be strong, go gently."

Stay safe,

– Matthew Wade, London 2021.

Contents

Prelude

The train pulled out of Dorasan Station. Electric motors whirring into life as the wheels slipped and shuddered, searching for grip on the steel tracks.

The lights in the cabin momentarily dimmed as the power was sent to the motors, an effect often seen in the older electric trains.

Sparks flew as water and leaves got in between the train and rails, lighting up the grey block buildings as it went trundling past.

It was a busy service, with standing room only in the standard carriages, and all of the first-class cabins taken up.

Most of the passengers where business commuters on their way home, with a smattering of tourists taking advantage of the new open borders between the two halves of the nation.

As the platform disappeared from view, the young Korean looked out towards his old home in the North. How its grey concrete buildings stood in uniform rows, and flags of the old regime could still be seen flying from the windows.

It was a cloudy day, and the air had a crisp bite to it. Passengers on this train had all been wearing long coats and fur hats as protection against the cold, but as the train moved out of the station, the heaters filled the carriages with warm air, stale from the old vents that were in need of a clean; a metaphor for the old North Korean state – scratch below the polished surface and you will find dust and decay.

The station was situated a short distance from the southern border between the North and South, on what used to be the old demilitarised zone; and as it approached the boundary, the crow's nests of the guards' gun turrets still filled him with awe and wonder. And fear. For that was their purpose, as much as housing a gunman; they were there to strike fear into the hearts of anyone who dared cross the line.

But those turrets were now abandoned, much like the North itself. The promise of a new life and freedom beckoned, and many fled as soon as they were able. Declarations of love and loyalty to their leader were quickly abandoned in favour of the new world order. It's funny how devotion and dedication can disappear with the puff of freedom.

The train was heading south, final destination; Seoul. In the mind of the young Korean, still the enemy. A symbol of the growing spread of capitalism, and the decline of morality and discipline.

In the old world, citizens would not be allowed to be loud, or disruptive, or disrespectful to their superiors. Now it is practically encouraged; leading to disorder, chaos, weaker minds, and ultimately a weaker nation.

Now Hollywood films were being shown – uncensored – in cinemas across the North. Young people's minds were being polluted with the disease of ideas. Thoughts of greed, lust, and capitalism were spreading quickly. All these things prevent one thing from happening. Progress. They are all distractions to the hearts and minds of ones who would otherwise follow and obey and serve their country for the better.

There could be only one solution to all of this. And it would not be too late to stop it.

His thoughts were interrupted by a knock on the glass. The young Korean looked up as the sliding partition of his passenger compartment opened, and in stepped the American.

The American was wearing a modern ski jacket and gloves, with a beanie hat and sunglasses to complete the look.

The young Korean struggled to hide his contempt for the man. His swagger and bravado suggested that he was in charge, and showed his lack of respect for order and uniformity, and above all it showed he had poor manners.

To confirm this, he was chewing gum. A habit perpetuated by the west, and creeping into Korean society as much as the other ideas were. He watched as the American masticated loudly, not bothering to show him the courtesy of closing his mouth when he chewed, the slapping and smacking sounds turning his stomach.

The young Korean gestured to the seat across from him "Gyo u i sin."

The American sat down on the bench seat opposite the Young Korean and placed a laptop on the table between them "Sa gun i chung," came the response.

The American stripped of the coat, hat and gloves, but left the glasses on.

Always trying to look cool, thought the young Korean. *Vanity; one of the diseases of the west.*

"Do you have the agreement?" the young Korean asked, struggling not to just lean over and wrap his hands around his throat then and there. Anything to stop the awful chewing noises.

The American opened the laptop and turned the screen to face the young Korean "This is the final draft that they will sign in London."

The laptop had a document open that had the seal of the President of the United States at the top, and the words *Top Secret* printed in red, diagonally across each page.

The young Korean sat and read the text on screen for a few minutes. As his eyes scanned the page his brow furrowed in concentration and distaste.

The American was watching him as he read through, glasses remaining on; hiding any expression from his accomplice. When the young Korean got towards the end, his eyes widened, and he looked from the screen to the American, and back again. "Is this true?" he asked.

"Yes, comrade, it is the proposed agreement. McDonald will announce it to the world next month in London, and it will be signed shortly after."

The young Korean stood up and laced his hands behind his head. "This is impossible. We cannot allow this to go ahead. He must be stopped." He looked down at the American. "*You* must stop him."

The American laughed. "You think *I* have the power to stop him? I am a pawn. I have no authority." The American paused, contemplating. "You must call our mutual friend in the North."

The train sped south through the countryside towards Seoul, the outskirts of the city coming into view. The old block concrete buildings were disappearing, and being replaced by modern, glass skyscrapers festooned with neon lights.

The young Korean picked up his phone and dialled. After a beat, he spoke. "I am with the contact at the moment, the situation is… dire. Our worst fears have been realised. McDonald must be stopped."

He listened for a while and spoke a few words of agreement here and there.

"Yes. I understand." His final comment as he hung up the phone.

"Our mutual friend asks if you have any other power to help us in our quest?" He addressed the American.

The American shifted uncomfortably "I have given you the document. You have a lot more knowledge than you have now." The young Korean could see his reflection in the American's sunglasses. "What more can I give you?"

The Korean thought for a moment. "You are correct; my apologies. You have given us what we require. As much as you are able to be of use. Now your work for us is done." He dialled another number and spoke into the handset in Korean. He placed the phone back on the table as the bright lights of city came into view. The door slid back and two other men entered the carriage. At this point the young Korean man stood to leave. "These two gentlemen will take care of you from now on."

"What is this? You getting rid of me now?"

One of the two men quickly clamped a handkerchief to the American's face, and the protesting stopped.

As the train sped its way through towards Seoul, people drank in bars and laughed in the streets with the carefree abandon that comes with living in a free city. As the last of the evening sun disappeared behind the skyline, a large bundle in a plastic bag was thrown from the rear of the train, bouncing and tumbling across the tracks before coming to a stop.

Part 1 – A Sunny Day

One

I have a confession to make. I'm standing on the steps looking over to the lawn outside Winfield House, London, and it is immaculate. I mean, not just cut well, but flawless. I have played pool on worse surfaces.

It's as though the grounds keeper's life depended on getting every blade of grass exactly the same height, which is probably not too far from the truth. OK, so not his life, but probably his job; and therefore, the happiness of his good lady back at home. So, yeah. Like I said.

As I look out to the midday sun, my eyeline reaches a good half an acre until it ends on a perfectly straight row of trees separating the garden out back from the cityscape beyond.

Skyscrapers can be seen lining the treetops, with office workers milling around in their thousands as the glass surfaces are cleaned by men suspended in a cradle, and are slowly lowered through eighty or ninety stories as they wipe down the glass.

There is a low rumble of traffic and the occasional honk of horns that has become the soundscape to many a metropolis, and London is no exception. Every so often a shout would echo up, reflected by the buildings. Always the same thing, builders yelling at each other from up some kind of scaffolding tower; bike messengers screaming at busses as they are carved up on the roads, or the screams of school children as they play out in the early morning sun.

Two perfect flower beds are to my left and right, both bordered by an immaculate hedgerow and the flowers themselves look like they came straight out of a florist's magazine photoshoot. I wonder if it is the same guy that does the lawn that also does the flowers? No, stupid question. They must have a small army of people doing just the flowers.

I have already decided that when I retire, I'm gonna try and get a lawn like that. And a flowerbed to match.

I will spend all day doing nothing more than just tending to a garden somewhere and have no stress other than to worry when to water and when to just let them be.

It's a beautiful sunny day and looks like it will turn out to be a hot one. Not great if you are standing in the sun in a black suit and black tie. I have my standard issue wrap arounds on, but they just shield my eyes from the glare (and hides my line of sight from any potential threats). Let's hope the sun lotion lasts and I don't get burned to a crisp today.

Anyway, all these thoughts are a deliberate way of distracting me from what I need to confess.

I'm nervous.

I'm nervous of the day ahead, and all of the things that can go wrong. I'm nervous of personally screwing up. I've gone through all of the training, but this is my first time 'in the field' so I have a lot to learn; and learn very fast.

The only blot on the landscape is in front of me. Breaking up the perfect English garden is the flying fortress know as Marine One; the president's impressive "Nighthawk" helicopter, that has just landed in the centre of the lawn, kicking up dust, earth and grass as it descended.

If I were the groundskeeper, I would be upset by the sight of my manicured stripes disturbed in such a brash way. Even more upset by the inevitable tram lines left by the aircraft skids once it takes off. How do you work those out of the grass anyway? Brush them back up? Use a divot repairer? Who knows?

But now POTUS has touched down and it's time to focus.

A line of fully charged black limos has pulled up on the gravel path in front of this impressive manor house.

They are heavily armoured Cadillacs, specially commissioned for the job. Loaded with the latest tech in urban warfare, telecommunications and luxury. 'The Beast', as they are known to the public, are some of the most expensive and impressive executive protection vehicles on the road today.

The rotors of Marine One are starting to slow as the pilot kills the engine, just as the door opens and a set of steps drops down onto the grass (another dent for my guy to fix).

President McDonald cuts an impressive figure as he strides across the Winfield House lawn. He is flanked by four Secret Service agents set in a 'V' formation, as well as the secretary of state, the first lady, vice president and the chief of staff.

One of the agents, Peters, walks over the far side of the second limo in the convoy and opens the door, just as the president approaches the car.

The president pauses to kiss the first lady gently on the lips – a move he is known to do for camera over the years – and she is accompanied into the house by the secretary of state and the vice president.

He is assigned a randomly different car in the convoy each time he travels, and today is Beast number two.

The rest of the agents are moving into position, scanning around them as they open the doors and step into their own vehicles.

I am moving too, getting into car five, at the rear of the convoy.

As the door closes, I nod at the agents sitting around me.

To my right is Special Agent Salanski, an experienced agent in the field with over fifteen years' service as an agent to the presidents he has served under. Before his tenure in the Service, he was awarded the congressional medal of honour in the North Korean war of '86, and hand-picked by the chief of staff to serve under Davis. Salanski is watching me as I buckle my belt and fumble this simple task as I nervously locate the strap to the lock.

As he punches me in the arm, he tips his Ray-Bans down his nose. "Relax, rookie. We all get nervous on our first time out. I remember Turner here when it was his first time. Sweated so much you couldn't be downwind from him for more than a couple of seconds," he said as he laughed heartily at the stoic looking black man opposite him. "Ain't that right, Pepe?"

Special Agent Turner hardly flinched at Salanski. "Don't call me Pepe for nothing."

For a heavy set, muscular man, Turner took the joke remarkably well. I guess that is what all agents of the service will tell you; camaraderie goes a long way. If you can't bond with your fellow agent, then you have no place working alongside them.

The car broke out into laughter. The two agents up front turned in their seats as the four in the back fell about.

"Hey, rookie, you'll be OK, just stick with us and we'll show you the ropes," said the driver, Special Agent Stevens.

Just then my earpiece crackled into life. "Pocahontas is in the carriage. Roll out."

All five Cadillacs moved forward at the same time, the seamless acceleration well-coordinated, as the guidance systems kept them all exactly three feet from each other.

As I glanced over the shoulders of Robertson and Turner in from of me, I could see Stevens in the driver's seat. He held onto two joystick-style controls either side of the wheel, which operated 360 cameras covering all angles of the car, projected onto an HDU in front of him.

The driver's window was covered in camera angles, data and a live feed from the control centre, known as the operations room (located inside of Winfield House) giving a navigation route to follow, with an alternative should the need arise.

The other side of the glass showed news feeds from the local news stations, and right now, it was covering the front of Buckingham Palace.

Special Agent Li was scanning the images as he caught me looking over at him. "You OK, Doc?"

He was looking at the camera feed that showed the rear of our car, with the four of us sat in our two by two facing seats. In the image I saw the other three turn to me as Li asked his question.

"Yes, sir. Just keen to get going."

"Good to hear, Doc. Looks like we could be in for a busy day," he said as he gestured toward the screens.

Li spoke over the earpieces. "All agents, switch on watches and locate." All of us tapped our wristwatches, activating the GPS trackers we all wore. Our names all appeared on the head up display in front of Li, overlaid on a map to show are locations, and our vital health statistics.

All of the men in the car had green or amber next to their pulse, blood pressure and injury details. All except mine, of course, which were showing red across the first two.

"We are all in this together. Remember that and you'll be fine," Li said to me as he surveyed the charts.

The news channel was now showing a helicopter feed of central London, panning out and back toward the Mall, where hundreds, if not thousands of people lined the streets behind crash barriers. The camera zoomed in a little to show the depth of the crowd. In some places it looked to be thirty people deep, maybe forty.

The image cut to a young female reporter who was standing on the road just in front of the barriers. Only Agent Li could hear what she was saying, but it was clear that she was referring to the crowd behind her as they cheered and waved their Union Jacks as she turned to wave at them.

The image then cut to a studio with a male host talking seriously to camera, and an image of a Korean man appeared on screen. It was a blurry picture, but I recognised the tattoo of a flower across his neck almost immediately. It was the face of the leader of 'The Flowering Knights', or the 'Hwarang'. An active terrorist cell operating out of North Korea, who until recently, had seemingly gone into hiding until recent events in China alerted the US intelligence to their resurgence.

The illusive leader, sometimes referred to as Gim, (from Gim Won-sul, the second son of the first century Silla general Gim Yu-Sin) has been spotted in South Korea, Mainland China and, more recently, central Europe and Turkey.

Agent Li visibly stiffened when he saw the report. "Let's hope those flower boys don't get any ideas about interfering today." He spoke to the window, but the other men in the Beast murmured their ascent.

The convoy rolled out of the front gates and onto the Outer Circle. It is a road that cuts through the perimeter of Regent's Park and is a single lane edged by hedgerows that separate the tarmac from the park. It is truly a gentle and peaceful place to be.

As soon as we pull out onto the road, a squad of police motorcycle outriders flanks our convoy; sirens whirring and lights flashing. My peace is immediately broken.

The convoy starts to speed up. A pair of joggers coming towards us on the opposite side of the road stops and takes a photo on their glasses – the tell-tale hand gesture up to the side of the face gives it away.

As the lead car starts to accelerate harder, the other cars (including ours) in the convey follow the same instruction and stay exactly 3 feet from the car in front, electric motors whirring up to a high pitch whine as the acceleration pushes me back into my seat.

These cars may be heavily armoured, and heavy in weight, but they can accelerate a fast as any sports car on the market today.

"How you doing, Doc?" asks Stevens as he catches my grip tightening on the leather arm rest between me and the door.

I turn my head and give him a dead pan response "A-OK, sir," I say as I can feel my pulse quickening. Not the typical response to give, but it seems to satisfy my colleague.

We swing a left onto Park Road. A leafy street with two lanes each way, flanked by rows of old-style terraced houses, each one worth way into the millions. I catch myself thinking about the type of person who lives in these places as we power down the road. To live here you have to be from money, or at least have made enough to afford such an exclusive address. Location is the selling point, as they say.

We overtake a group of three cyclists and a dog walker on the pavement side. The lead rider flips our convoy the bird as we sail past.

"Did you see that, guys?" says Salanski as he grins out towards the window.

"First of many, my friend," calls Agent Li from the front. "First of many."

As we make swift progress down Park Road, our police escort powers ahead to stop traffic as we reach our first major junction. At this point we can choose to take one of several routes to reach our destination. In the Service we call this the 'Diamond'. In other words, the start and end points of our route are fixed, and in this case, known to the public, but the route we take can vary from anything between a direct route 'as the crow flies', or spur off in a wider arc to curve to our destination, making a diamond shape on the map.

In extreme cases, the convoy itself may split up, throwing and potential assailants off the scent by sending some cars one way, and some the other. Not the ideal scenario, as it means we have less cars in the convoy, and so each one is more vulnerable. But sometimes extreme tactics are necessary

Today we are taking the direct route, as most of the general public knows where we are going. As I glance at the window in front of Agent Li, I can see the news feed is showing a bird's eye view of our cars taking a right onto George Street, and the left that takes us onto Great Cumberland Place. Another single lane road with high terraces homes, restricting the views of the city either side of us.

So much for secrecy I think to myself.

As I look at the image the camera pulls back to show us approaching our first big landmark.

Marble Arch sits at the front of Hyde Park like the gatekeeper of yesterday. A monument that once stood at the entrance of Buckingham Palace, moved centuries ago to its final resting place in front of us – only British Royal family members and the Royal Horse Artillery are permitted to pass underneath. So, in keeping with Royal tradition, our cars with the American flag flying swoop around the monument and head down Park Lane.

It seems as though our news anchor is having the same thought, as she is showing images of the king, and cutting to a map that shows our route to the palace in real time as we move down it.

"So much for the element of surprise," Salanski remarks as we accelerate once again.

This is when I start to see the crowds forming. At first it was the sight of steel barriers along the edge of the pavement that caught my attention. But now as we start to drive past Hyde park to our right, people are beginning to gather to get the first glimpse of us, and the many other dignitaries that will pass through this morning.

"Ok, here we go guys. Keep 'em peeled," says Li. His steadfast expression never leaving him.

The crowds are made up of a variety of people. Most are casual observers; onlookers who happen to pass by as we hammer through, innocent bystanders who naturally turn as the sirens speed past.

Some are supporters of the various international parties, or the British institution, and wave flags, signs and other souvenirs in support.

They are not the ones we are looking out for. Our senses are tuned into any threats that may be in the throngs.

In fact, the travelling international convoy is one of the Secret Service's worst nightmares. We have not got the protection of the White House, and, whilst abroad, rely on foreign security arrangements and local police forces to support us. In a world where trust and need to know is paramount, this is far from ideal.

As we continue down past the Royal Parks, the crowds become much thicker. Now there appears to be a mix of friendlies and no so friendlies. I can hear the jeering and booing from inside the car, and so can my fellow agents.

"Hostiles in the crowd." The voice comes over our radio earpieces.

The next sounds made me jump. A pop on the window to my left has me turn to see an egg oozing down the glass, the broken shell sticking to the broken yolk as it slides down out of view.

"Eggs thrown. Stay on course," says Li.

Then there is a bang on the roof.

"What was that?" says Salanski.

Turner points out of the rear window from his position opposite. "Looks like a rock." I turn to see the object skimming off the rear of the car and dancing down the road like an out-of-control football.

At that point my earpiece voice comes back to life. "Problems en route ahead," comes the command.

Li is now making hand gestures to manipulate the head up images on the windscreen in front of him. I see him zoom in and out of the helicopter feeds of us, and the ever-thickening crowds ahead. As his right hand continues to move in and out, we can see the problem up ahead.

Anti-government, NATO and American protesters are swelling up against the crash barriers up ahead on Constitution Hill; the road that takes from where we are now straight to Buckingham Palace.

The crowd are fifty, or sixty people deep, and nearly all of them are chanting in unison. I can't hear what they are saying, but I can see the rage in the faces. Gone are the pro-American and British flags, and they are replaced by banner with slogans such as 'Feed the people', 'Stop the wars', and 'Kill the rich'.

Suddenly, the camera cuts to one section of the street. The barrier has burst open and people are pouring onto the road. The crowd is numbering in the hundreds, and they are running down Constitution Hill, toward Hyde Park Corner. Towards where we will be in about thirty seconds.

"Route B! Repeat, route B!" comes the voice in my ear. Just as we approach the four-lane sweeping roundabout of Hyde Park Corner, we swerve off onto Piccadilly. A much longer route that will have us making our way around the 350 acres of the park, allowing us to cut back down towards the Mall.

This is doing nothing for my heart rate, and I try to concentrate on my breathing, trying to relax.

A high-pitched whine appears from both sides of us. A motorbike pulls up alongside our motorcade, a rider at the front and a guy on the back holding a camera. Several flashes momentarily blind me as he tries to take a picture inside rear of our car. "Paparazzi on our 3 o'clock," barks Turner. The first time he has said anything since we left Winfield House, but now in full battle mode.

He pulls his gun from his holster and simultaneously powers down his window. He points the pistol at the motorbike, who quickly swerves, regains control and backs off.

"Busy day already," says Turner.

I twist around in my seat, trying to get a better view around the car.

"Hey, Doc," says Salanski. "Relax. This sort of thing happens all the time. The press can get quite aggressive."

"Crowd to our right," points Turner as he winds the window back up. A mob roughly thirty strong is running on an interception course toward us. From the distance I could see that they were carrying baseball bats, rocks and were wearing scarves to cover their faces. Not good.

I could also see that they would not make it to us in time to cause any damage.

"Hostiles not an immediate threat," reports Li.

Our police escort blocks the traffic as we accelerate down towards Green Park Station. Workers, tourists and recreational joggers stop and watch as our motorcade carves a path through the streets of the city.

Buckingham Palace is situated on the south east corner of Green Park. It is 830,000 square foot of opulence, and the finest furnishings, staff and comforts that the world can offer. Dating back to the British monarchy of 1850, it stands as a focal point for the Royal Family and state gatherings in times of mourning and of celebration.

We had turned at Green Park and headed straight down the perimeter lane of the park to meet up with the Mall. A picturesque street that leads in a straight line from Trafalgar square, right to the face of Buckingham Palace. ·

A gap in the barriers had been created for us by the local police so we can join the Mall right in front of the Royal residence. As soon as we emerge from the Park, all of as gasped at the sheer volume of people.

All the way down the Mall and Constitution Hill was what could be described as a sea of people. There were families with children on dads' shoulders, groups of international students on holiday taking pictures, supporters dressed in their international colours, including some pearly kings and queens. But also, I could see the hostiles. Banners as before, but now we were up close, there was jeering, booing, spitting, and some unpleasant hand gestures. Lines of police were spaced out on the streets facing the crowds, and already they were pointing and shouting at members of the throng as more eggs, stones and anything they could find started hitting our car.

I knew that there were plain-clothed officers planted in the crowds, too. And, sure enough, as we exited the park and slowed on our approach to Buckingham Palace, I witnessed two officers arresting a man by pulling his arms behind him and cuffing him as they frog-marched him away.

The front of the palace is guarded by a great statue called the Victoria Memorial. It is a giant marble obelisk on a roundabout where the Mall meets Constitution Hill. A statue of the late queen sits underneath a giant golden angel known as 'Winged Victory'. But now, behind the carving is a large rectangular marquee, with arena style seating housed inside. The press pit.

Sitting behind the memorial, and facing toward the palace, the world media had all eyes trained on the front of the royal building ahead.

Around 150 seats were crammed into this small space, with clusters of media outlets comprising of three or four people from each major news station around the world. Each section seemed to follow the same pattern; a tech sitting behind a bank of screens and a small mixing desk, controlling the camera feeds and sound, some kind of director or producer shouting directions to the anchor standing out front with a microphone in hand and their back to the palace.

Each reporter had a camera trained on them, often operated from the shoulder of another staffer wearing a pair of headphones, with one eye glued to the viewing lens and one eye searching around for any activity on the large stage set up in front of Buckingham Palace.

The stage in question was set up behind the great black gates that protected the courtyard of the palace from the crowds, and comprised of a row of seats lines up at the back, with a dual podium front and centre. A row of thirty-five flags were flying behind the stage; thirty-four for each member country and the main NATO flag in the middle.

To the left, and lower than the stage was the bandstand. A drummer, bass, guitars, horns and strings were present, with a conductor facing them, nervously fiddling with his baton as he watched the stage to his right.

As our motorcade circled around the arc of crash barriers between the crowds and the winged monument, Li agitatedly barked out instructions.

"Sir, I would advise against it—"

"Yes, sir, but I do not recommend—"

"Yes, sir. Understood, Mr President, sir."

The motorcade was already slowing to a stop.

"POTUS wants to meet the crowds and shake some hands. Direct orders. All agents out immediately."

Our doors sprang open as all of us stepped out of the car and onto the street.

The first thing that hit me was the noise. It felt like an air pressure – a wave of an invisible force hitting me as I stood and faced the people. There must have been a thousand or more right in front of me and more stretching back further than I could see.

The next thing that struck me was the heat. After a drive in an air-conditioned car, the warmth and the smell of thousands of people under this scorching midday sun felt like a warm waft from the beach, albeit with a staler odour of bodies that had been standing around in a tightly packed bunch for a couple of hours.

The door of car two sprung open, and out stepped McDonald, already with his arm in the air waving, and a beaming smile that came so naturally to him.

"Snipers in position," came the confirmation in my ear piece. Without looking I knew there would be at least ten men on the roof of the palace, with scopes trained on the people in front of us, just waiting for anything threating to pull the trigger.

McDonald strode toward the crowd, glad handing, high-fiving and fist pumping the screaming fans. The master of the people.

He leant back against the flag wavers for selfies, as several of the agents rushed forward every time a hand reached out a fraction to far, or someone reached into their jacket pocket for their phone.

A particularly excited woman grabbed the side of his head to pull him closer; her lips purses, ready to plant a slobbery one on the commander-in-chief's cheek, but Turner was there in a flash. Swatting her hand away with his left, and yanking McDonald back a pace with his right by a tuft of the suit coat in the small of his back.

McDonald laughed a belly laugh, slapped Turner on the back and flashed his wedding wing at the slightly wide-eyed woman. She relaxed and played along, blowing him kisses as he moved on.

"Leather jacket dead ahead," came Li over the earpiece.

As I looked up, I caught sight of a pink rubber mask being pulled down to cover his face. A grinning cartoon pig.

"Hey, fuck you, McDonald!" The man lurched toward the barrier, one leg trying to find purchase as he pushed himself up and over. Heavily tattooed hands outstretched in a C-shape. Ready to grab and crush.

He vaulted up and over, lunging as he went. McDonald was turning to see as the man got to within three feet of him. Three feet closer than most get.

A flash of suit and Salanski – a former NFL draft hopeful back in the day – body slam tackled him six feet in the other direction. The other agents formed a wall between the president and the crowd. A wall of patriotic steel. No one gets close.

Salanski was cuffing the man on the ground, ready for the meat wagon as noise made me jump.

"Gun!" I shouted.

The other agents sprung into a circle formation around the president, hand on holsters.

"Relax, rookie," said Li as he pointed toward the palace.

The two large screens showed a group of people walking up and onto the stage. They were led out by the Royal family, the king, his wife, Queen Jessica, and the Duke and Duchess of Cambridge, Phillip and Eleanor.

The family were followed by world leaders from the UK, Europe and all of the NATO members, save the US, who was still standing in the street taking selfies.

The cameras panned over to the band, whose tympani player had let a series of drums ring out, as the conductor waved his baton to start the Music for the Royal Fireworks, the great Handel composition written in Royal celebration in 1749.

Also, when played over a loud PA system, the source of my phantom gunshot.

"Looks like we are being given the hurry up. Feeling frisky today, fellas?" asked McDonald as he straightened his tie for the cameras.

Without waiting for a response, he started off in a slow jog toward Buckingham Palace, head held high, with a confident yet relaxed look on his face.

The agents all fell in line behind him, a group of suits with black shades and curly earpieces, jogging along beside him.

I glanced up at the screens and saw the image. Behind us were the convoy of the presidential motorcade vehicles, along with the motorcycle outriders with full flashing red, white and blue lights flanking the wings.

My god, the president looked powerful at this moment. I stole a grin as I realised what a showman he was. With the day full of NATO summit activities, including this lunch with all of the foreign leaders and the British Royal family, this image was going to be the one that makes the headlines. He knew what he was doing all along. Fashionably late. Make the king wait for him, and give him a show of power to boot. Damn, this guy has balls.

As the president mounted the stage, we followed suit and flanked the wings.

McDonald went along the line and shook hands with the leaders and was greeted like an old friend by King Henry.

Henry IX was a young king. Coronated when he was just eighteen, Henry Frederick, along with President Joyce McDonald, was the leading figure in the new pan European, Asian and American treaty, following the fall of the communist state in North Korea.

Now at the age of just thirty-five, he had formed a long friendship with McDonald over the negotiations of the treaty, and helped pave the way to a demilitarisation of North Korea and a start of a new elected government.

This summit was to be the showpiece meeting. The icing on the cake of the last few years' hard work, and a final statement to the communist world; the US and the UK were in control.

McDonald took his seat behind the king, who stepped forward to the podium.

"Your Excellencies, ladies and gentlemen.

"On behalf of The Royal Family, and the British people, Jessica and I are delighted to welcome you to Buckingham Palace for this lunch to mark this historic NATO summit.

"It is a tremendous pleasure to see so many heads of state, ministers, business leaders and friends from across the globe here today.

"And I extend a particularly warm welcome to our new found friends from Korea, and President P'il Songhyon, whom I have formed a strong friendship with over these past three years."

A noticeable mix of boos and cheers wafted over the crowd ahead.

"As I stand here today, I reflect on the journey we have all taken. It was only three years ago that we sat in negotiation room with the people of North and South Korea, and negotiated the Pan Korean Treaty, that brought peace and democracy to the region, and allowed for a new found freedom for the people of Korea, allowing them to live their live as they want, without the fear of oppression or violence from their leaders.

"And I've been left in no doubt about the optimism and ambition that people of Korea have for their future."

More cheers and applause rose up.

"The continent is home to one of the world's fastest growing economies. And across the region there is a palpable urgency and determination to grow.

"Twenty million jobs must be created each year across the region to meet the demands of young people entering the labour market.

"Harnessing that enthusiasm, and ensuring that it leads to environmentally and socially sustainable growth and jobs, is why you have all gathered here in London for this NATO Summit today."

He gestured to the world leaders standing behind him.

"It has been encouraging to hear about the productive, long term partnerships that have been developed at today's Summit, as well as the increasing investment from UK businesses into Korea.

"These investment partnerships will help to create quality jobs for young people across Asian countries and here in the UK.

"And most importantly, your collective effort is helping to generate the private investment needed to meet the UN's Global Goals. These goals will ensure that we see a safer, wealthier, better educated, healthier, more equal and greener world by 2090."

He once again turned to the leaders behind him.

"I know that today you have mainly been discussing financial investment. But let me end by saying that I hope we can also boost investment into Korea's natural environment.

"Asian countries have some of the most abundant, valuable ecosystems in the world, relied on by millions of people for their livelihoods. It is always deeply worrying to hear when those livelihoods are threatened, for example by the illegal wildlife trade, extreme weather events, or by the current devastating locust plague in the South of Seoul.

"At the start of this new decade, and as we lift our ambition towards the climate change conference in New York later this year, we must all work together to invest in the natural world – our most precious asset.

"And we must ensure that the growth ahead is used to protect and repair the delicate balance of nature.

"People quite rightly expect the coming decades to bring a rise in living standards.

"It is in the interest of the entire planet that Korea shows us all how to deliver growth and jobs, while also leading the world in the fight against climate change.

"I'm confident that the partnerships you have agreed today can be at the heart of this vital mission."

This seemed to be the most popular statement yet, judging by the crowd's reaction.

"But there is still much work to be done. The threat of military action from the region has, in the past, been very real, and I thank my fellow heads of state for their tireless efforts in bringing stability to Korea, and a new hope to forge lasting partnerships between new found friends."

He paused and looked out to the crowds.

"It is also wonderful to see so many of you out here to support us in our endeavours, and I thank the British people, and citizens from around the globe for their messages of support and goodwill."

More applause.

"Once again, Jessica and I, the Duke and Duchess of Cambridge, have been delighted to welcome you to Buckingham Palace today.

"We hope you have an enjoyable day."

A rumble of applause rolled across the people lining the streets, as Henry handed over to McDonald.

As the president and king crossed over, they embraced, and McDonald stepped up to the podium.

"Thank you, Your Royal Highness; your excellencies; ladies and gentlemen. Today marks a landmark in world politics. Not only are we celebrating a newly joined Korea, but a new path forward in peace for the nation.

"Today, in this NATO summit, we will be discussing the further way ahead, not only for the region of Korea, but for the rest of the world, as we harness our new found friendships, and work together to overcome global issues such as the climate, global healthcare and sustainable growth in labour, housing and food industries.

"But today marks more than that, as with the blessing of the senate and the house of representatives back home, and permission from the Royal household here in the United Kingdom, I will be setting out a new plan to—"

I stood and waited, the voice had stopped, but the president was still talking. The sound had cut out. A chorus of booing emerged from the crowd.

"Seems we have a power cut," said Li in my earpiece.

I looked up and, sure enough, the screens had gone out. But something else had changed. I couldn't put my finger on it at first; it takes time to notice what isn't there.

Sound.

The low rumble of traffic. It had reduced considerably. But more than that. The constant hum the makes up the background noise of modern cities. The hum of air conditioning, machinery, motors.

"Power is out across most of the capital," came Stephens' voice, who was monitoring the situation from the Beast. "Surveillance is out, looks like all network connections are down. Car and local radio signals still running, but no power on the grid."

A distant bang rang out from the crowd. Something was happening far away, down the Mall. Seems as though there was trouble. I could see a section of the crowd moving, pulsing, like a wave. Trying to get away?

"Confirmation required on shots fired on the Mall." Again, in my earpiece.

"Negative. That was a big smash on the roads leading up to us. All traffic signals have gone out as have all electronic signage and navigation. This ain't no normal blackout."

Before the response came the screens crackled back into life. The crowd gave a sarcastic cheer.

McDonald was still playing to the camera, giving a 'What can you do' gesture and looking from the press pit to the jumbotrons above.

But then a new face appeared on screen. It was a man sitting in some kind of sandbag enclosure, with a symbol of a flower and a knight behind him. He was sitting down, and standing behind him were two men wearing balaclavas and holding machine guns. The flower tattoo on his neck was unmistakable.

"That's Gim. Somebody shut this off!"

Gim, the leader of the active terrorist cell operating out of the former North Korea and a strong opponent of the treaty to unify North and South Korea, was somehow on the big screen at Buckingham Palace; with the world's media watching.

The press pit. I hadn't noticed that until just then, that they still had power. Little red lights on the front of all of the cameras told me that they were still filming.

Someone had stage managed this intervention well.

"Good afternoon," boomed out the voice.

"I thought I would give my own address to the world. One that you cannot ignore."

Technicians were frantically racing around behind the stage, trying to pull the plug.

"As you may have noticed, I have just taken control of London's infrastructure." He paused to let this sink in, as the crowd grew restless.

"I am now in control." He continued. "You will now all listen to me." His face looming over the stage below.

McDonald tried to speak on the mic, but nothing came through. Gim continued. "You westerners make me laugh. So caught up in power. So preoccupied in world domination that you fail to see the simple truth – it is you who is reliant on power. Simple power to run your daily lives; and without it – you are crippled."

The buzz in the crowd was growing to a panic.

"Now, I have control of your precious electricity that you need to charge your cars, or run your banks, or even open your doors." This caused audible shouts and gasps from the audience.

"Yes, you are finally realising that even something as simple as opening the doors to your homes requires access to the infrastructure that I now control." He grinned at this statement, knowing the effect it was having on the people watching.

"So. What to do about this… situation."

Technicians were shouting at each other behind the stage.

"I have a simple set of requests." Continued Gim. "Three in total. Three requests that I hope will be taken seriously."

McDonald had stopped clowning around, and was now shouting at aids to stop this before it could carry on any longer. But to no avail; Gim carried on.

"Number one. NATO and the US cease all activities in North Korea and withdraw troops immediately."

McDonald and the other world leaders were watching in disbelief on stage. McDonald himself was turning crimson, losing his cool exterior.

"Number two. McDonald himself will meet with me and publicly acknowledge the Hwarang as a political group and member of the Korean assembly."

The world leaders were starting to wave and shout at each other. Pointing at the screen as they did.

"Only then, will I consider giving you back control of the city. Failure to meet my demands will result in more serious consequences." He leaned into the camera, making his face even larger on screen. "You think this is bad, McDonald. Just wait and see."

Li was back in my ear. The other agents were also receiving the message as they all had pressed a tell-tale finger to their earpieces. "Get ready to move out. Pocahontas to return to lair. Repeat, return to lair."

There was a squeal and a ringing sound through the PA system. The face on screen was speaking once more.

"I will allow you to speak, President McDonald."

McDonald grabbed the microphone at the podium. In a slow and controlled voice, he looked at the press pit and said, "The US does not negotiate with terrorists."

He turned to his side and looked at one of the techs punching buttons on the consoled. "Now get this worthless piece of crap of the screens."

Gim smirked on his screen image above. "You use strong words, McDonald, but you see I have the power here."

"Stevens, bring the carriage to the party," said Li in my earpiece. "Ready to roll."

McDonald started to speak, but no sound was coming through.

"You see," continued Gim, "I am the one in control here. And just to show you I am serious, how about a display of power, as you seem to love them so dearly?"

The screens cut away from Gim's face and to one of the news copters circling above.

"You westerners love the technology," he gloated, "but it will be your downfall."

As the camera tracked the copter, it circled above Green Park, and swung back toward Buckingham Palace.

The screen cut back to Gim's face. "I will give you one more chance, Mr President. Do you accept my requests?"

McDonald spoke, audibly again through the sound system. "The US does NOT neg—"

"Oh, you are so predictable. So be it."

The image returned to the copter. For a while it hung in the sky as before. Then the camera zoomed in a little tighter. As it did the audio from the pilot came over the feed.

"Hey – looks like we are on camera folks… What…?" he said as he tapped buttons in front of him. Then the lights in the cabin went out.

He flipped a few switches above his head. "Switching to manual," he said. His voice calm and measured.

The rotors of the helicopter appeared to momentarily slow. The pilot pumped at the throttle, his voice rising a note. "Losing power," he said as the whirring of the engines died down.

The then rotors slowed more.

"We've lost all power," he said as he tapped his earpiece. "Mayday, mayday we have lost power. Repeat, lost all power."

His voice came over in my own ears, as did the alarming response, "All engines are down. Initiating emergency power up."

The cockpit lights flickered, and then turned red. The head up displays in the cockpit came back online, but with minimal information. They were running under emergency protocol.

The helicopter was starting to lose altitude, dropping to within striking distance of the palace, the image of the aircraft on screen was not much bigger than the viewable helicopter itself, the pilot wrestling for control in the skies over London.

All faces in the crowd were looking skyward, many hands moving up to cover mouths.

The helicopter starting to climb once more, the rotors speeding back up.

"Regaining control. Looking for a spot to make an emergency landing."

Then all the lights went out.

"Mayday, mayday! Power out!" shouted the pilot. "I've got nothing."

The next moment happened in slow motion for most watching. Although it, in reality, took only a few seconds.

The rotors slowed to a stop. The helicopter hung in the cool summer breeze for a moment, suspended in time as the world held its breath. Then it headed down. It dropped like a stone let go from the roof of a high rise. Never turning or rolling, just dropping straight down.

The pilots voice could still be heard over the speakers.

"Brace for impact. Brace fo—"

The copter slammed into the roof of Buckingham Palace, with a deafening crunch, sending dust and debris skyward.

A scream of panic rose up from the streets as hundreds of people started to run away from the building. The front rows were the first to move, but the rear sections wanted to get a closer look at what had happened, so started surging forward.

The centre was experiencing a dangerous crush. Parents started hoisting children up above their heads to protect them, and some fell down, trampled underfoot as the panic rose up.

The world leaders on stage tried to appeal for calm, but without any sound, they were powerless.

"For god sakes, get the sound back up, man!" shouted King Henry. "People are getting hurt out there."

Police were trying to calm the spectators, but a few hundred uniforms were no match for a panicking crowd. They were simply overwhelmed.

I looked on in horror, feeling equally powerless to do anything, my earpiece was full of the noise of barked instructions from Li, but all were hopeless.

Then a noise rose up from the crowds. Distant at first, but rapidly growing in volume. Chirping, music, ringing.

The crowd quietened. The waves of pulsating bodies slowed to a stop as all of them reached down to pockets, touched their glasses, or put hands into jackets and bags.

Behind me, aids and guards of dignitaries did the same. Phones.

All mobile phones as far as I could see were ringing at once. My own back pocket began to vibrate.

I looked around me and my fellow agents were all tentatively reaching for theirs. I shrugged at Li and Salanski as they swiped the screen and put theirs to their ears.

"Hello, people of the world." I looked around me for who could be making the call. In front of me, thousands had their phones pressed to their heads, but were starting to look up and point at the screens behind me.

I turned to look, and Gim's face had returned to the big screens.

"As you can see, I am deadly serious in what I say. Every time I do not get the answer I like to hear, I will give you another display of power."

The two gunmen remained stationed behind him on screen. "I have one more request to go," he said as you could hear a pin drop anywhere in the city.

"Your new announcement you were about to make. I would like you to not make that statement and destroy the associated act you are about to pass."

He smirked at the camera once more. "Or do I have to give you another display of power?"

McDonald, still standing at the podium, repeated what he had done before, starting down the camera lenses, he spoke clearly and precisely.

"The US. Will NEVER. Negotiate. With terrorists."

He looked at the king behind him, and turned back to camera.

"Mr Gim. You have crossed a serious line. Now it is my turn to set demands. One. You will end this attack on these innocent people. Two. You will surrender to the US where you will be given a fair trial in our court system under the accusation of war crimes, and crimes against humanity. Three. You will cease all activity of the so-called 'Hwarang'. If you do not comply immediately, you will be met with deadly force."

Gim gave a macabre chuckle as he spoke. "Mr President, you underestimate me. You have always underestimated me. And you are incorrect. It is you who will be met with deadly force."

The screen turned off.

Phones were disconnected, and a murmur began to rise from the crowds.

At first is sounded like crying, whopping, a mixture of both. I couldn't make out what I was hearing. Then it grew louder.

It sounded like a war cry. A shriek. A scream rising up from the streets in front of us like a demonic chant, a tortured scream of souls. All I could hear was it in unison, like the people were possessed.

It was a cry of "Aelilililil!"

A repeating, relentless scream. Like some ancient civilization had been reborn in front of our very eyes.

As I looked down Salanski appeared beside me "What in God's name is going on?"

A significant number of young men in the crowd had donned masks. Pigs.

I scanned left and right. Hundreds, maybe more were donning pig masks.

"Get out of here! Pull back! Pull back! All agents secure POTUS and head to the Beasts, rear of stage. Repeat. Rear of stage. As soon as POTUS is secure move out."

We all sprang into action. Li and Salanski grabbed McDonald by the arms and made to move hm away.

Below us, and down the Mall, the war cry reached a crescendo.

"Aelilililil!"

"Aelilililil!"

"Aelilililil!"

Men in pig masks were attacking the crowds with baseball bats, rocks and fists. Men, women, children, old and young were all targets. People who tried to run were cornered and beaten.

Riot police started to move in.

I took one last glance at the scene before turning to face McDonald and the other agents.

It looked like a bad war film. Some kind of horror was unfolding like a scene from hell. Screaming, bloodshed and panic had ensued. We need to get out of here. And get out of here fast.

As I took a step forward, I moved across the stage to accompany McDonald and the other agents, when I saw one of the Korean security detail grabbing what looked like a hat on the top of his head, as he pulled down with his left, I saw the distinctive pink of the pig mask.

I glanced down at his other hand, and saw a flash of metal.

"Gun!" shouted Li. The standard phrase for an armed assailant.

Li lunged forward and turned to embrace McDonald, his back toward the shooter. Salanski drove forward to put himself between the shooter and the president, making himself big like a bear – a counter intuitive reaction that has to be learned through years of training.

The shooter was fast. Turner drew his gun as the pig man fired. Turner fired back. Turner shot three times in rapid succession. Each shot hit the shooter. The first hit him in the chest, the second and third in the forehead.

The dum-dum bullets were designed to have no exit through the body, as to not strike any innocents behind; and in this case, the Duke and Duchess of Cambridge who were being wrestled away by their own security detail.

I must confess that I froze. This was my first time out in the field, and I had never seen a man die before (well, at least, not in such a violent way).

The man had crumpled to the floor. I could see the hole where the bullets had penetrated the mask, and a pool of blood was beginning to leave his head, spreading out over the stage.

I was standing behind McDonald, who still had Li standing in front of him, protecting him, with his hands on his shoulders.

I stared transfixed at Li as he removed his shades to look at me. "Doc. I need…"

Li coughed and blood trickled out from his mouth. He slipped down onto his knees as McDonald tried to hold onto him.

I rush forward to the pair, as did Turner and Salanski. Li fell forward onto the floor, and Turner rolled him over.

"Agent down! Agent down!" he shouted as reinforcements arrived in the form of medics from behind us in the palace.

I moved over to Li and put my hand on Li's neck. I shook my head at Salanski. "He's dead." My voice caught in my throat as I passed my hand down over his eyes to close the lids.

I looked up at McDonald who was being steadied by Turner. "Mr President, sir, are you OK?"

Blood was on the front of his shirt, which I had assumed was Li's. But as he spoke there was a hoarseness to his voice.

"I'm OK. Just…" he coughed and a spittle of blood came up to his lips.

"Agent Li took the brunt of it."

A screech of tyres made us turn to see our cars pulling up in front of the stage. We dragged McDonald down toward the open door as another pig faced man in a suit appeared to our left.

"Gu— " I started to say; my senses coming back to me.

I was cut short by the sniper bullet tearing through him. Without taking a moment to pause, Turner and I bundled McDonald into the car, with Salanski in close pursuit, and the car sped away as soon as the doors closed.

I leant over to the front of the president, and, without asking permission, pulled open the front of his shirt to revel a small puncture wound just above the mid sternum.

"Open my med kit," I commanded the car. A drawer opened under the seat and my field kit appeared.

I opened a bandage, tape and sterile dressing and began to patch up the wounded man.

"Report," said Salanski.

"Single shot entry wound, possibly clipping the lung with no exit. Patient will survive with immediate medical treatment."

"Marine One. Now," said Salanski.

Stephens touched the panel in front of him. "Pochohantas en route to base. Emergency protocol Zero, Delta, Alpha. Repeat. Zero. Delta. Alpha. President down."

As the car tore through the streets of London, I struggled to keep my balance on my knees on front of the president.

"Sir, is Marine One wise? The news copter— "

"Secure network, agent," coughed McDonald. "They can't hack us there." He coughed up some more blood again and leaned forward to speak to me.

"Give it to me straight. What does it look like?"

"You will be fine, sir. I have enough medical facilities on board Marine One to repair this."

McDonald fixed me with that famous stare he had given so many reporters.

"Liar."

"Sir?"

"Don't bullshit me, agent. I can feel it. I think it hit my heart."

The car screeched into the entrance of Winfield House, and straight onto that immaculate lawn. This time not caring for its upkeep.

As soon as we exited the car, we put McDonald onto stretcher and hoisted him aboard the chopper, engines already spinning up.

Marine One is the call sign given to any United States Marine Corps helicopter that carries the President of the United States.

This was a Sea King helicopter, equipped with a full office, telecommunications centre and medic bay. If required, the president can run an emergency meeting with all White House operatives from on board.

We went straight to the medi bay.

Once there, I strapped McDonald to the gurney as we lifted off.

I pulled out the mobile body scanner, which could see inside the president's body, and help me assess the damage done.

As I looked on at the monitor, he looked at my face.

"I have spent many days across the table from seasoned negotiators in North Korea, China and the Middle East. And I can tell you that you have the worst poker face of them all."

I looked back at him and swallowed. "Sir?"

The scanner started ringing out its emergency siren, to tell me what I already knew.

Salanski was standing behind me, his skin glistening with sweat.

"What's happening?"

"He's going into arrest." I punched a few buttons on the console.

"Do something." McDonald's voice was only a whisper. "Anything. That's an order."

I hesitated. My hand over a syringe in the drawer.

"What is that, Hill?" asked Salanski.

"Nano tech. It could help him. But— "

"Do it! He gave you an order!"

"It's experimental. I am only one of the few people to trialling it."

"You mean you have it in you now?"

"Yes, but— "

"Are you dead?"

"No, I— "

"Then do it!" Salanski spat out the last word, and pulled his gun out of his holster. "I am bound to protect this man in front of me. He gave you a direct order. Now inject him or I shoot you." His voice was deadly calm.

I picked up the syringe and first connected it the console.

"I'll have to program it first," I said as I connected another cable to a hidden chip on the side of the syringe.

A loud alarm sounded in the cockpit. Salanski opened the medibay door and looked toward the cabin in front. The other agents were strapped into the luxury seating, and the cockpit door was open with the pilot visible.

"They are firing at us. Surface to air missiles. Deploying flares."

Salanski came back and stood beside me.

"Whatever you do, do it fast," he said. "We need to land quick and get to safety."

"Thirty seconds," I said.

The screen in front of me was loading up the program. The timer was counting down to zero.

A loud explosion rocked us off our feet, I barely kept everything connected.

"Flares caught the missile. There could be more."

I watched as the counter ticked down to zero. "Data uploaded," I said as I unplugged from the console and held up the syringe. Its blueish liquid shimmering under the helicopter lights.

I leant down and inserted the syringe into the now unconscious McDonald.

Another boom, this time shaking us more violently. I flew to the ground, banging my head as I went down. My vision blurred as I tried to stand.

"Another missile. We need to land and get off. Now."

I stood back up next to my patient, the syringe was rolling on the floor, a trickle of blood seeped out where the needle had gone in. I crawled under the floor as it rolled away from me, catching up with it as it clipped the side of the desk. I went back over to McDonald and straightened it up against his skin and inserted it into the vein.

I pushed the plunger.

We watched anxiously as the screens registered the new injection.

"More incoming!" was the shout from the cockpit. This time a loud explosion shook us more deeply than before and sent us into a violent spin.

"We are hit!" came the pilot's voice.

The gurney the president was on flew across the room, tipped and he fell sideways, still strapped to the deck.

Everything was spinning faster and faster. Alarms were sounding in the cockpit as I looked out of the window to see we were in a flat spin.

We were surrounded by black smoke, and the ground was coming up to meet us fast.

"Brace for impact! Brace for impact!"

We span faster, and faster, falling.

Down we went, the English countryside approaching fast. I could see a road, and cars, then houses. We were seconds away from hitting.

I glanced up at the president as he lay unconscious on the gurney. The computer readout read 'Success'.

I looked back out the window as the ground was in touching distance.

There was a gasp as McDonald opened his eyes and took in a breath.

I let out a primal scream as I realised there was no escape.

I closed my eyes and—

I was back in the rear seat of the Beast.

Two

I jumped out of my seat, banging my head on the roof of the car, and yelped.

"Woah! Slow down, Doc!" said Salanski. "What spooked you?"

Li turned around from the passenger seat. "What's up with him?"

I was starting to hyperventilate. I was breathing hard in and out, but my chest felt tight, like there was an anvil weighing down on my lungs. "I think I'm going to be sick." I was scrambling for the door, and found the handle.

"What are you doing?" Salanski had my arm.

"I want out! I want out!" My heart was racing, it felt like it was about to burst out of my chest. My whole body was tingling with adrenaline, but I felt like I was about to blackout.

"Salanski, get him out. We can't have him like this. Pull over," said Li. He spoke into his wrist mic "Car five pulling over – medical emergency. Cars one to four proceed as normal."

We pulled to a stop and I yanked the handle and bolted. We were on Park Road when I exited the car. Three cyclists and a dog walker had just gone past, the front rider flipping the bird to the convoy that was now disappearing into the distance.

"You OK, Doc?" asked Salanski as he studied my face. "You're freaking out. Just slow it down a second."

I was standing on the road, bent over with my hands on my thighs, just focussing on my breathing. Next to me was a grassy bank. I raced over to it and dry heaved.

OK, I thought to myself. *Don't panic. There will be a logical explanation for all of this.*

I was already trying to cook up the reasons why this was happening. Had I eaten something and experienced a hallucinogenic trip? Was I simply dreaming? Was this just a vivid dream – and still ongoing?

"Salanski? Will you slap me round the face please? Good and hard?"

"Doc?"

"Just… I had a vivid dream. Just need to snap out of it."

I was expecting more protests from the agent, so when he hit me, the pain shot through my jaw. Definitely awake.

"Thanks."

"Any time. Now are you gonna let me in on what happened in the car just then, or can I keep slapping you?" He gave me a grin that said he was joking – well – half joking, trying to relax me.

"Can we walk and talk?" I asked. "The fresh air is helping."

Salanski turned back the way we came. "Well, our ride is long gone, so we better head back to Winfield House. It's about five minutes this way."

He put his shades back on as we started walking.

I tried to relax by taking in the view of the beautiful parks, and warm sunshine, and waited for my heart beat to slow down to something like normal.

"I had such a vivid hallucination," I began. "We had made it to Buckingham Palace and the speeches had started. Then we were attacked."

Salanski gave me a sideways look. "Attacked. Attacked how?"

"Gim."

He pulled his glasses down to look over them at me.

"He appeared on the big screens. Hacked into them somehow. Hacked most of the London infrastructure. Brough traffic to a standstill. Brought down a news helicopter down onto the roof of the palace."

"Sounds extreme."

"There's more. A rouge agent – don't know who – shot Li and McDonald."

"OK, now you are scaring me."

We had stopped walking and had turned to face each other, just near the entrance of Winfield House.

"Just a dream though, right?" Salanski was searching my eyes for an explanation. I stood and closed my eyes for a moment. The sun felt good on my face.

"And this all happened in the car. Just then?" Salanski was still trying to get an answer from me. Years of government training meant that he couldn't let things go.

"Yeah, I—"

A distant noise penetrated the air. The band had struck up the opening chords to 'Music for the Royal Fireworks'.

My pulse quickened once more. My head turned back to where we had come from.

"What is it, Hill? You look like you might throw up again."

I took a series of deep breaths in and out. "That was the song. The song from my dream." I wiped my forehead, but realised my palms were covered in more sweat than my brow.

"Pfff. They always play that one over here. The Brits are practically brought up on it." Salanski took his shades off and put them in his top pocket. "Come on. Let's go back to the house." He threw his arm over my shoulder in a brotherly way as we strode up the gravel path. I just wanted to lay down somewhere or throw up. I couldn't work out which at this exact moment.

Three

Winfield House from the inside is even more spectacular than from the outside.

The house was largely red brick, with uniform cream-coloured edgings on the corners of the building. The three sets of windows in the centre were cream to frame the entrance, which was a large white windowed door surrounded by marble arches, overlooking the expansive terrace.

The interior was like a hotel. High ceilings and light cream walls gave a backdrop to gold edged curtains and a marble relief designs on the walls, all set off by American flags standing to attention on golden poles, with oil paintings and photographs of former US presidents hanging on the walls.

As we walked up the path and into the grandness of the entrance hall, I could see and hear a hive of activity around me.

Agents were moving from room to room with purpose. Black suits were everywhere. Analysts were often accompanying them. They were the techs, the ones who would sit at a computer all day long and advise the guys in the field. You could spot a tech due to their attire – normally jeans and a hoodie – but also as they were normally buried in paper. Not looking up but down. As opposed to the agents, who were always on guard. Always vigilant. Always watching people.

We turned a corner and walked into the main operations room, where amongst the terminals and people, an elegant black woman in a smart suit was standing behind the desks, watching the news footage on the large screens on the far wall.

Special Agent Gina Del Fonte was the head of the field operations at Winfield House. Admired and respected throughout the White House; she was in charge of the team looking after the president whilst he was in London.

She was with McDonald right from the beginning of his presidency as a senior agent, and took over as head of operations when she showed great aptitude in the Korean tour as an intelligence operative in the US military, where she headed off three separate attacks before they got to the commander-in-chief.

But she really made her name by her work ethic. Growing up in a bad part of town, she had to work even harder than her white male counterparts to even be on equal footing, something she still campaigns verminously against even to this day.

She was the first woman to head a task force in the White House, and the first to lead the Secret Service in the field.

She also had a reputation for being brutal. If any one of her agents weren't cutting it, or were seen to be slacking off, she would give them the hairdryer treatment. That is to say, she shouted so loud in your face it felt like a hairdryer.

As we entered the room, she turned to face us. I tried to gauge her mood, but her face betrayed nothing. She must be a poker player.

"Doctor Hill."

She walked over to me, and before I could speak, put her hand on my arm. "First of all, are you OK? I heard there was some kind of medical problem?"

Her face broke into an earnest look that told me she genuinely cared.

"Yes, ma'am. I'm fine. Just had a panic attack. First time in the field."

She paused and contemplated my answer for a moment. She, like all of the agents I work with, and have ever worked with were always searching for more information. "Do you need medical assistance, Doctor?"

"No, ma'am."

"Good, then you and Agent Salanski can help in here." She gestured up to the monitors where King Henry was making his speech.

My god. I thought. *It's exactly the same. The positioning of the people, the press pit, the band stand, even faces in the crowd I recognise.*

"McDonald just pulled a stunt," said Del Fonte. "Got out and started shaking hands with the crowd. Can you believe that? Had to jog up to the palace when the Royal family got pissed waiting for him and almost started without him."

Salanski chuckled. "Wow. That's a big move. Got lucky there. Could have gotten nasty. This what you saw in your hallucination, Doc?"

I was speechless. The answer was yes, but I couldn't bring myself to say it.

The king was wrapping up.

"…and I thank the British people, and citizens from around the globe for their messages of support and goodwill.

"Once again, Jessica and I, The Duke and Duchess of Cambridge, have been delighted to welcome you to Buckingham Palace today.

"We hope you have an enjoyable day."

"Here we go, everybody," said Del Fonte, as McDonald stepped up to the podium. "Track the crowds, track the near and mid distance."

"And the podium," I blurted out. That was rewarded with a few sideways glances.

"Thank you, Your Royal Highness; your excellencies; ladies and gentlemen. Today marks a landmark in world politics. Not only are we celebrating a newly joined Korea, but a new path forward in peace for the nation..."

My heart was pounding inside my chest. This was all too real. I could feel the rising panic once more. It was like some horrific car crash, or a fight in the street. You know you shouldn't stare; you don't want to, but you just can't help but look.

"…Today, in this NATO summit," continued the president, "we will be discussing the further way ahead, not only for the region of Korea, but for the rest of the world, as we harness our new found friendships, and work together to overcome global issues such as the climate, global healthcare and sustainable growth in labour, housing and food industries.

But today marks more than that, as with the blessing of the senate and the house back home, and permission from the Royal household here in the United Kingdom, I will be setting out a new plan to— "

All the lights went out. Del Fonte and most of the people in the room were looking around at each other.

"OK, stay calm, people," she said. "Just a technical. Emergency backup kicking in."

The monitors in front of us cycled back up, to reveal Gim's face grinning down from the palace above McDonald.

The otherwise quiet analysts and agents jumped out of their chairs, and grabbed keyboards and phones almost instinctively.

Gina's eyes were ablaze. "What the hell is going on?"

"Not sure, ma'am. Coming from the palace screens."

"Ops – trace where this is being broadcast from. Li, come in. Li, can you hear me?"

"Looks like comms are down," said an analyst.

Salanski grabbed me by the arm. "You said in your dream Gim came on the air and hacked the power. Is this what happened?"

Del Fonte turned to hear. She maintained her professional air, but the mood had changed. The caring side had vanished.

"What do you know, Doctor – what was in your vision?"

"I… Gim comes on the screen like he is now. Then he sets demands… McDonald refused to comply. Then he brings a news chopper down onto the roof."

"What, wait. He brings a chopper down?"

Most of the analysts in the room had stopped and were listening to our conversation.

"You also said that Li and McDonald are shot," said Salanski.

"What? Doctor, as head of this operation you must tell me everything. Do you have inside information we need to know about? How are they shot? Tell me what happens?"

"It was just a dream— "

"Tell me everything." The room had fallen silent around us.

I took a breath and spoke. "Some of the crowd put on masks. Masks to look like pigs. The crowd started rioting. Then as we were leaving, masked man appeared from behind us; possibly one of the Korean security detail. Li tried to protect the president, but the bullet went through both of them."

"Wooah, wait – you mean McDonald is shot? Doctor Hill, you had better come clean on all of…" she waved her hands towards the shots of Gim at the end of the room "…on all of this. What is your involvement? How did you come by this information? Why was I not informed at the earliest opportunity?"

Salanski had pulled his gun. "Start talking some sense, Doc."

Gina gestured for him to lower his weapon.

"You said they were shot – were both killed?"

"Negative. Li died on the scene. I tried to help McDonald on board Marine One."

"And were you successful?"

"Unknown. We were shot down before I could tell. That's where the dream ended. But it was just a dream. Probably fed by watching the news about Gim and the summit late last night in my room." I forced a smile, but it did nothing to convince my hostile colleagues.

We were distracted by the events unfolding in front of us.

"Look!" said Salanski. He was watching the news feed on the screens; the image showed the helicopter.

The pilot's voice came over the audio "Mayday, mayday! Power out!"

The footage focussed in the pilot, and its two other occupants – the camera operator and reporter, and then zoomed out to show the helicopter's rotors slowing.

The wide angle showed then plummeting on a collision course to the roof of Buckingham Palace, snipers previously hidden were seen running out of the way as the chopper slammed into the palace. The sounds of the crowds screaming as it hit.

The noise inside the operations room had dropped as most of the people now stood and gawped at what they were seeing unfolding.

The screen cut to a news anchor, obviously getting a feed in his hear to cover whilst they worked out what they could and could not show.

"It appears. Yes," he said, touching a finger to his earpiece, "yes, it appears that the terrorist known as 'Gim' has infiltrated the London power network, and, yes, I can confirm," touching his earpiece once again, "this is so awful, one of our reporters and the pilot from this news channel were on board the helicopter. We are trying to get people on the scene to confirm if they are still alive, but I'm afraid it doesn't look good."

Del Fonte was looking at me, eyes widening. "Doctor Hill – you have exactly ten seconds to explain yourself!"

"I— I have a dream – a vision of these events— "

"And what exactly did this *vision* of yours tell you is going to happen next? You said Li and McDonald were in jeopardy?"

"Yes, ma'am. In my dream, palace. A shooter in a pig mask— "

The screen cut back to the palace, where the image showed the roof smoking, a black, acrid smoke, and a small fire starting to spread from the base. I could see the snipers had run for cover, and were standing on the edges, the flames too hot for any of them to get near.

Gim then came back on the screen. I was distracted by a vibration in my jacket pocket. *Of course. I had forgotten that detail.* I pulled out my phone. "Joel," I said to the hoodie wearing man in front of me.

The lead analyst looked up as I handed him my phone. "Quickly, track the incoming signal. It's Gim."

He plugged my handset into his computer and fired up a piece of software.

All of the people in the room had their phones to their ear as Gim spoke the words that I had heard before.

"Hello, people of the world." Gina looked over at me, her expression hardened.

"As you can see, I am deadly serious in what I say. Every time I do not get the answer I like to hear, I will give you another display of power."

The line went dead. The Joel Thomas turned in his chair and shook his head. "Call was too short, and the signal was encrypted. Sophisticated stuff. Sorry."

We were watching the stage again. Gim's face looming like some kind of boss in a video game over the president's head. McDonald now looking very powerless as he stood and watched like the rest of us.

"Get a message to someone. That guy to the right of the Korean President. He is the shooter. He has a mask in his back pocket, the rebels in the crowd are about to be instructed to riot…"

As I said it, it was playing out in real time. The camera cut to the crowd where it seems hundreds of people were in masks and starting their attack. An uncoordinated attack with the pig masks lashing out at anyone who was within reach, and frightening to watch. Even more frightening from above.

"Joel." Everyone, including the head analyst was glued to the screen. "Mr Thomas."

He snapped out of his funk. "There must be a way they are communicating that is different to the phone call we just received."

Joel rubbed his chin as I thought about the detail I was missing. "There was no second call."

"Sorry?" said Joel.

"The rioters in masks must have received an instruction, but none of them looked like they received a call."

"So it was a text, or an app of some sort."

"Right. Can we trace the source of that?"

The beard scratching carried on. "If I had a phone with it on then yes. Nowadays texts or messaging services have meta data imbedded that is almost impossible to conceal. Meant to stop terror cells communicating." He shrugged his shoulders. "With the app on a handset. Piece of cake. Could give you the location of the sender to within a few metres. But without it…"

He was distracted by the scenes in front of us. The volume had been turned up and we could hear the now familiar screams and cries of the crows as chaos ensued.

My heart sank. "This is it – McDonald is about to get shot." I was hanging on the back of the analysts chair as I watched the chaos unfold.

The agents all rushed their delegates off stage, as in the melee, a gun flashed as Li raced at speed to protect his President. The speed it all unfolded was so fast, I hardly registered it, even though it was the second time around.

The cameras zoomed in on McDonald and Li, as Li lost his grip on the president's shoulders and slid to his knees. He looked like he was prostrating himself in front of his leader, McDonald trying in vain to hold him up. But as he fell sideways and crumpled to the stage floor, I could see the light had gone from his eyes.

I stood and ran my hands through my hair. "I saw all of this." I turned to Del Fonte and Salanski. "I knew this was all going to happen."

As soon as the words had left my mouth, I regretted it. Del Fonte acted without hesitation.

"Doctor Hill, I am arresting you on suspicion of terrorism charges, and plotting to assassinate the President of the United States of America. Officers, place this man in custody."

Two police officers appeared at my side and slapped on the handcuffs. I didn't struggle as I was escorted out.

Four

The newly refurbished Paddington Green Police Station was home to some of the country's most dangerous terrorists. The centre contained a series of holding cells, or custody suites, where prisoners could be detained indefinitely, under new terrorism laws.

Government legislation over the last few years had tried to change the law to allow a 'no contest' arrest and detention, which meant that police would have powers to arrest and detain on any suspicion of terrorist activity.

The government tried to pass the act through without public knowledge. However, it was leaked out to social media, and, understandably, lead to a public outcry that caused a U-turn in government policy.

Little did the public know, though, that the law was passed a few month later, and now Paddington Green was a place where people were left to rot.

Some had been there months, some years, and, without possibility of trial, seemed likely that their lives would end there too.

As I was escorted down the corridor, I was met with a mixed response. There were a lot of cat calls. "Hey! Fresh meat! Why don't you come over to my place later!" and "Love the suit, pretty boy!", as well as prisoners jeering, making howling noises and banging their cell cage doors.

The guards paid no attention as we walked down the slab grey corridor. I, on the other hand, could feel my pulse racing once more.

But it was the ones who were quiet that scared me the most. One guy who must have been six three and built like a wall just stood and stared at me. As I walked by, he drew his finger across his neck.

Please God, let this nightmare be over.

The guards pushed me into an open door and slammed it behind me without saying a word.

I was alone in my own cell. I had a bunk bed, a sink and a toilet in a ten by eight room. But I was safe. For the moment at least.

I sat on the bed and stared at the wall in front of me. I slipped off my jacket and kicked off my shoes. They had taken my tie, belt and laces from me when I was booked in, so I lay back in just trousers and shirt.

I put my hand over my eyes and began to sob.

My thoughts were interrupted by the lock turning and the door opening. Two guards stood in the doorway as a third brought another man in. "Little company for you," smirked one of the guards as my new roommate was pushed roughly inside.

The door slammed shut once more and I looked up at the new arrival in front of me.

Something about him looked familiar, but I couldn't quite put my finger on it. I looked him in the eye and then down his body to his hands. *Tattoos. Could it be?*

Before I could say anything then man reared back is head and flared his nostrils, sucking in air in a snorting motion.

He spat a ball of mucus into my face, its warmth running down my cheek.

I shot up to a stand and pushed him back with my chest, squaring my shoulder up to him.

"I don't like you," said the man in a broad London accent. He was staring me straight in the eye, an unspoken game where the loser was the first to break contact. Luckily the Secret Service trained us in how to deal with guys like this.

"I have been trained by the US military, in advanced hand-to-hand combat. I served years in Korea and dealt with the militia deep inside the Korean jungle. And you think I'm going to be intimidated by little schoolboy games of stare down?" I was always good at making myself sound better than I was. True. I had had some hand-to-hand combat training, but as a doctor, I never had to use it. In fact, the closest I got to a jungle was when we flew in to assist wounded troops. Even then, I never left the safety of the helicopter.

The man laughed and broke eye contact. "You're lying, mate. You don't seem the type to be good in a fight." He pronounced it *foiyt*.

"Just try me." My confidence overshadowed my ability.

This seemed to make him seethe even more. He puffed up his chest and then cracked his neck to the side.

"Now here's what's going to happen," said my roommate. "I'm going to get out of here soon. But before I do, I'm going to have some fun with you. See, I don't like you Secret Service types."

My eyes widened at this statement.

"Yeah – you heard. I can spot you a mile off. The hair, the suit, the shoes. Stinks of government. Of the service."

I stared him down. His glare never wavering. "You were in the crowd. Jumped and attacked us."

"So what of it?"

"You think you are special, don't you? Think if you hide behind a mask you are invincible." I was getting hotter, my heart pumping harder. "Well, I call bullshit on you. You are just a scared little boy."

As I spoke those last four words, I jabbed him in the chest with my finger, emphasising each one in rhythm with my speech.

The man let out a noise, much like a cat who has just had its tail stepped on, but at a much lower pitch.

His right arm swung round to my temple, but I was able to react and block the blow. As I did his left slammed my in the torso, making me buckle and wheeze.

He grabbed my head from behind, and slammed it down onto the metal railings of the bed, my vision exploding with stars.

I rolled onto my back on the bed, a waited for the next assault. I felt his hands grab my ankles and drag me onto the floor, my tailbone whacking the hard floor as I went down.

My head once more exploded as the force of the man's boot made contact with my temple. I rolled over onto all fours, and tried to stand.

"Haha! You look like shit, mate." The swagger in the man was apparent. "I know who you are. You are one of those American agents. Just like the ones who put me in here earlier today."

I stood my ground. "And I know you. Pig-mask-wearing coward who tried to attack the president."

The man spat on the floor. "Just following orders, mate."

I put a hand to my head and wiped away blood. As I did a hot, tingling sensation passed across the wound as my vision cleared.

"What the—" said my assailant as he stumbled backwards toward the sink.

I stood up straight and cracked my knuckles. I put my hand to my head once more, to check the blood was gone.

"You ain't right! How did you do that?" He pointed at me and backed away.

It was my turn to smirk. "There are things about me that you don't know. And attacking an agent of the US Secret Service is a criminal offence."

He looked around the cell and gestured at the four walls. "Looks like you just lost your job, mate," he said with a smirk.

He rallied himself and charged once more, this time ramming his shoulder into my stomach, sending us both crashing into the door.

At that point the guards were banging on the other side, trying to force it open.

I ducked and twisted, and got onto the other side of the room as the door flung open, and two guards and two orderlies wrestled us both to the ground.

There was a sharp scratch on the side of my neck, and my knees gave way.

I don't remember much of the next few minutes, but I was aware of being strapped down on a bed. The bed was moving. A trolley? A gurney?

I remember being outside briefly. At least I think it was outside. The sky was grey. No. Darker than that. Black. With smoke.

Now I'm being lifted up. Loaded. A door slamming. Movement.

I must have passed out for a moment, as when I came to, I was a lot more lucid, and in the back of an ambulance.

I tried to sit, but I was being held down. My wrists were cuffed to the sides of the trolley, and there was a brown leather belt across my chest.

"Welcome back, Doctor Hill," said a familiar voice to my side. I turned my head to see Gina Del Fonte sitting next to me.

We looked at each other for a moment, neither wanting to be the first one to speak.

She broke the silence first. "I had to get you out of there, Gibson. We are being evacuated."

My mind was spinning. I didn't know what to say. She saw the look on my face and rubbed her temples "You need to level with me."

She pulled back and waiting for my response.

"Evac? What's going on?"

She looked at me with a look of distrust, her poker face slipping. "Oh, you mean you don't know now?"

"Ma'am? I'm sorry, I— "

"Don't you 'ma'am' me. You knew way more than anyone could have known about what went down today." She looked out of the window to see where we were going. "Listen, Doctor Hill. We are about to leave London, and transfer you to a secure prison north of the city, where I can't help you. You will be on your own, Gibson, and no one will believe you weren't a part of this… this terrorist attack."

She leant down so our faces were almost touching. "Please tell me you haven't turned. Tell me you're not working for the Hwarang."

I went to sit up, but the restraints held me back. I looked her dead in the eye. "No. No I am not working for the

Hwarang, or any terrorist organisation. I am loyal to my country, loyal to my President, and loyal to you."

She seemed to believe me, as she leant back in her chair.

"The man in the cell just back there – he said he was following orders. He was the guys who jumped us in the walk about earlier today. He is the one you need to interrogate."

She let out a low whistle. "I mean – dreams? Visions? And you predicted exactly what was going to happen. What am I supposed to think, Doctor? Jeez, you sounded like Hart back in Korea. He kept saying he could see things happening."

That caught my attention. "Hart said the same things?"

"It doesn't matter."

"No, please I want to know."

She just shook her head. The ambulance bumped and bounced along as the sunlight dappled its way through the side window.

"All I know is that I lived through this once already, and I saw it all laid out in front of me, like the pages of a book." I tried to turn to face her. "I'm not crazy, am I?"

"Gibson, I— "

She was interrupted by a heavy explosion. The ambulance screeched to a halt. Drwers flew open as my trolley bumped against the far wall.

"Driver? What was that? Report?"

The ground shook, my head rattled against the gurney as a bright light grew from outside, growing in luminosity until it was a white ball, blinding to look at and burning in intensity.

"Ma'am I… oh my god… it's the p…"

I was back in the rear seat of the Beast.

Five

This time I just sat and focussed on my breathing. I was either losing my grip on reality, or this was some kind of waking nightmare.

I let the convoy roll on. I wanted to see if the same events played out again. Then I would know if I had truly gone mad.

We overtake the same group of three cyclists and a dog walker on the pavement side. The lead rider flips our convoy the same bird as we sail past.

"Did you see that, guys?" says Solanski.

"First of many, my friend," calls Agent Li from the front. "First of many."

The déjà vu was making me feel quite sick, but I just listened to the sound of the air coming in and out of my lungs and stared out of the window.

"OK, here we go, guys. Keep 'em peeled."

A pop on the window to my left has me turn to see the egg oozing down the glass. I watched with fascination as the same broken shell sticking to the same broken yolk slid down the same window.

Was that the exact same egg? I wonder. *Or just an illusion?*

"What was that?" says Salanski, reacting to a bang on the roof.

"Looks like a rock," said Turner. I don't turn this time, knowing exactly what it was.

Was that the same stone? Is it made from the same atoms, arranged in the same order, or is a totally new stone, conjured up for my entertainment by some invisible sadistic ring master?

"Continue en route," comes the command from Li in my earpiece.

I wonder if we will see the same crowds, and, sure enough, I see Li skimming through images of a growing hostiles further up ahead.

"Route B! Repeat, route B!" comes the voice in my earpiece.

I can feel the same bumps in the road, smell the same smells in the air. *Wait a minute...* I undo my collar and feel my neck. I don't feel any marks where my short-lived cell mate tried to strangle me. I do up my shirt and straighten my tie.

So even I have reset.

Does that mean that I have the same amount of food in my stomach, the same amount of urine in my bladder? I still feel the same level of alertness and adrenaline as before.

Am I just like the egg, oozing down the window over and over again?

Now the bikes appear.

"Paparazzi on our 3 o'clock," barks Turner. Still the first time he has said anything, and once again in full battle mode.

He pulls his gun from his holster and scares them off, as before.

"Busy day already," I say, getting in before he can.

He dips his shades down and winks at me. "You can say that again."

I stay motionless. *Breathe in. Breathe out.*

"Hey Doc," says Salanski. "You look relaxed. How you doing?"

Li pulls up the obs from our watches. Mine has less red than before, but still flashing warnings.

"You need to relax, Doctor," advised Li. "Too much adrenaline will make you jittery."

"The day has only just begun," I mutter under my breath.

Salanski slaps me on the thigh. "My boy is good – right, Doc?"

"Crowd to our right," I say without even looking out of the window. "Won't get to us in time."

Turner twists in his seat and sees the mob trying to keep up with us on foot. "Hey, You just Mr Cool today, huh?"

"Affirmative. Hostiles not an immediate threat," reports Li.

We carried on the same route, making our way through the perimeter of the park as before, and arriving at the front of Buckingham Palace.

I sat forward as we skirted the edge of the people, trying to take in all of the faces as we slowed for the cameras.

I struggled to remember if they were all the same, the déjà vu playing tricks with my mind; convincing me that all I saw was real, and yet as if I were watching some kind of twisted playback.

I could see Li listening in his earpiece, but only paid the smallest amount of attention to it, as I knew the drill.

The order came in to disembark and follow the president towards the crowds.

Do I just do the same? I think as the same heat and noise rush hit me. *What if I try something else? To break something in the universe by making a change? Does the sky fall in? Will we all vanish into nothing?*

The same woman grabs McDonald by the scruff, and tries to plant the same kiss on his cheek, Turner batting her away once more.

My senses are heightened. I know what is coming next. I clock him before Li comes over my earpiece. My blood is already boiling at the sight of him pulling a pig mask over his face. It was the same man. The same man who spat on me in my prison cell. The same man who kicked me in the head as I lay prone on the floor. My anger took over, and before I could stop myself, I was running at him as fast as he was vaulting the barrier. With the tail end of Li's voice still talking in my ear about a man in a leather jacket, I had intercepted him the moment he had a foot on the barrier, his tattooed hands making their reach out for McDonald.

I caught him squarely in the nose with my fist. If you are gonna mess with events, may as well make them feel good, right?

The man landed on floor face first, as Turner rushed over to cuff him.

"Great work, Doc," said Li in my earpiece. "That's the kind of man we need on the team!"

McDonald glanced over at me and nodded in appreciation.

A cool breeze wafted over me as I took another breath in. *Was there a breeze last time?* Maybe I'm standing in a slightly different place. Or the adrenaline is heightening my senses. I'm starting to doubt myself. But I knew what was coming next. And now I knew what I wanted to do.

Six

The band had struck up and we had jogged in formation towards the stage. The king was wrapping up his speech and my heart was in my ears.

I was looking out front, but also looking to my side. *Who is the shooter? Which one is he of the twenty or so security, or Secret Service agents of each nation? Or was he just a rouge who slipped past security?* Unlikely. Security was ultra-tight. You had to have been cleared months in advance to even get close to this party.

Gim was about to appear on the screen, the power had just been cut. No one had flinched yet.

The helicopter. Damn. I forgot about those poor bastards.

Gim was now on screen, giving his ultimatums to the president. Here we go. I felt a sudden rage that these poor innocent people were about to die for what? A show of strength? It made me sick and angry. No. *Enraged* to think that someone would just kill another human being just to prove a point.

There they were. On screen was the copter. The pilot wrestling for control, but to no avail. I stood and watched with a tear running down my cheek as they plummeted toward us and slammed once more into the roof of Buckingham Palace.

I used all of the will in my body to not just scream and run away, wanting this to end more than anything else, but my sense of duty and purpose remained; my curiosity wanting to see how this could end. And my just wanting to nail the guy behind it all keeping me going.

"Now, Mr President, shall we continue our conversation?" Gim smirked at the camera. "Or do I have to give you another display of power?"

McDonald, still standing at the podium, leant into mic.

"The US. Will NEVER. Negotiate. With terrorists."

At least I can save one life today. I looked to my left. *Who looks nervous?* All of them. *But who looks ready to do something? Who looks like they have to do something they are unsure of?*

To men next to the Korean president were looking around them more than most. One had his hand inside his jacket. *Is that my man?*

I moved slowly towards my target, sliding my feet across the ground, but keeping my eyes on the screen like everyone else, so as not to alarm the attacker.

Next, it was the phone's turn to give everybody a jolt. Whilst the city of London answered the same call, I used the chance to really look around.

Who didn't answer? Who was just pretending?

There!

One of the palace guards was on his phone, but didn't have the same reaction as everyone else. He looked edgy, shifting his weight from side to side and taking deep breaths. I took another step towards him.

"Mr Gim," spoke McDonald. "You have crossed a serious line. Now it is my turn to set demands. One. You will end this attack on these innocent people. Two. You will surrender to the US where you will be given a fair trial in our court system under the accusation of war crimes, and crimes against humanity. Three. You will cease all activity of the so-called 'Hwarang'. If you do not comply immediately, you will be met with deadly force."

Gim was about to sign off. "Mr President, you underestimate me. You have always underestimated me. And you are incorrect. It is you who will be met with deadly force."

The screen turned off.

The same war cry rose up from the crowd "Aelililililil!"

I moved over to the rear of the stage. I watched the palace guard I suspected. He caught my eye and put his hands down. *Have I just blown it?*

Then I saw him. Moving quickly from behind the Korean premier, hand already pulling the mask over his face, focus forward. It *was* one of the Korean security operatives.

"Get out of here! Pull back! Pull back! All agents secure POTUS and head to the Beasts, rear of stage. Repeat. Rear of stage. As soon as POTUS is secure, move out."

Li and Salanski went to grab McDonald by the arms as a lunged to cut off the assailant.

Below us, and down the Mall, the war cry rose higher.

"Aelilililililil!"

The gun flashed in the sunlight as I got to within four feet of him. He saw me as I rushed him and turned the gun toward me.

I pushed hard and leapt forward; arms outstretched to grapple him as he pulled the trigger.

It felt like a punch in the gut. I landed spread-eagle on the floor, the screams of people ringing in my ears.

I rolled onto my back and looked at the clear blue sky. For the first time I noticed a single cloud, moving across to obscure the sun, the cloud itself moving slowing, but the shadow racing across us to blanket me as I felt the life slip.

Li's face appeared above mine. "Doc? Doc" he grabbed me behind the head as I could feel others trying to put pressure on the wound.

"Doc?" he said as he melted away. It was no good.

I was back in the rear seat of the Beast.

Seven

This time I set off a second earlier, changing my angle of approach as I ran at the gunman. This time he fired two shots, one hitting me in the shoulder and spinning me around to face the palace, the second ripping through my stomach. The latter of those two bullets sending me back into the rear seat of the Beast.

OK, one more go.

The next time I tried sheer speed. Charging him down with brute force. He was faster than me, shooting me square between the eyes.

Every time I got hit, I would appear in exactly the same spot in the car, with it on the exact same spot on its route.

I had been through this at least five or six times now, each time edging a step closer to getting it right, but each time getting hit.

I tried to walk up to the guy early on, even as we walked on stage, but doing that just got me thrown out for interfering with the Korean Secret Service. Even when I tried to show that he had a gun, I was laughed at by the forces on both sides, even Salanski pointing out the fact that he was carrying.

It was time I changed tactics.

I waited for us to arrive on the stage, and rather than wait for him to make a move, I approached the Korean security detail.

I stood next to him for a moment, as the king gave his speech. And, without taking my eyes of the crowd in front, spoke my warning to him. "I know you plan to shoot the president after Gim has taken over the broadcast. Follow me now, and I won't kill you."

I made to lead him off the stage, but he was quicker than me. He moved back and headed down towards the front of the palace with me in pursuit.

In my ear Li was already watching. "Doc? Where are you going?" After I gave no response, he tried again. "Repeat, Agent Hill. Why have you left your post?"

I pulled my earpiece out and followed my target who was now walking at a pace away from me and out of the palace grounds.

He looked over his shoulder and quickened his pace as he crossed the road and ran along the edge of the crowd barriers.

I broke into a sprint to keep up with him.

He sprinted too. He was fast, and my legs were pumping as hard as they could to keep him in view.

He flew down the street. Snatching glances over his shoulder as he passed the thinning crowds who barely paid much attention to us as he turned down a side street out of view.

I pounded the pavement and followed the path down a narrow alley between the buildings and stopped.

I had lost him.

Where could he have gone? I could see the other end of the alley way and it was about a hundred, perhaps a hundred and fifty metres away. There was no way he could have covered that ground in the few seconds it took me to catch him.

No. He must have gone in one of the doorways.

I moved down the alley until I came to the first one. I tried the handle. Locked.

I moved slowly down to the next, checking my lines of sight as I went. Movement in the window above me. I froze and put my back to the wall.

I waited as long as I dared. People were milling about in the street beyond, but nobody was walking near me. I slowly leant forward, scanning the first level as I moved.

Movement again. This time I held my gaze for a beat longer. The window was closed, so I darted forward to the next alcove in the wall.

The next doorway was a few paces forward. I moved my hand out slowly, inching it moment by moment towards it whilst snatching glances up as I moved.

I turned the knob. It creaked as it moved, and I was able to ease the door inwards.

I had opened it enough for me to slide up to it and move inside.

I placed one foot across the threshold and stepped up the small step as I pushed the door wider.

He came at me with explosive force, coshing me over the head with the butt of his pistol as he powered me down to the pavement and raced on down the alleyway.

My head was fuzzy. I put my hand to my head and felt the open wound where the blood was oozing out of.

As I started my run to catch the agent, a tingling sensation passed across my head, and my vision cleared, and my head felt instantly fresh again.

We appeared out of the alleyway into a busy London street. People were out shopping, drinking in bars and eating in cafes on the cobbled streets.

Most of them paid no attention to me, or gave no clues to my target, by paying no attention to him.

I scanned the scene in front of me and saw the man I was chasing. He had removed his jacket, and had it hooked on one finger over his shoulder. He was strolling down towards one of the cafes, casually looking in shop windows as he went.

I needed to flush him out. I reached for my badge and held it out in front of me. "US Secret Service. Freeze."

That's how you get a crowd's attention. The people around me turned and watched as I moved towards the Korean.

"Sir. US Secret Service. You are under arrest under the United Nations Terrorism Act."

Tourists had pulled their phones out and had started filming our encounter. A quiet rumble of a murmur had risen up around me. As a young woman passed in front of him, she glanced up at the commotion. Trying to steal a glance of the scene as she went about her day. As she passed near the Korean, he grabbed her by the arm, swung her in front of him and pulled his gun out and forced it against the side of her head.

The people in the immediate vicinity scattered and formed a large circle at our periphery, many still holding up their phones as we stood off on the cobbled streets of London.

Don't people get the danger of a man holding a woman hostage with a gun? You people care more about your social media ratings.

I was still holding my badge out as we stared each other down. The woman he had taken hostage was sobbing as she shook in front of him.

"US Secret Service. You are under arrest. Put down the weapon and give yourself up."

He cocked back the hammer on his gun.

"This is your last chance, put down the gun…"

"Or what?"

He had a heavy Korean accent, and pronounced it as *ar wha?*

"You Americans are all the same. All bravado, but I see you have no weapon. Any closer and I kill her. Then I kill you."

I took a step forward, knowing the ace I had up my sleeve.

A loud bang came from behind us that elicited a scream from the crowds.

The helicopter. I closed my eyes in grief.

The Korean was smiling. A smile that spread across his face, moving from ear to ear as his shoulders shook up and down, and the smile turned to a chuckle, then a laugh.

I balled my fists in rage.

"You see, American. We have already won. The plan is already in progress. Soon we will detonate."

A breeze blew through the streets that kicked up dust and litter.

"You mean there is more planned? After the blackout?"

The Korean stopped laughing. "How do you know about that, American? How did you find out?"

Now it was my turn to smile. "I didn't, but thanks for the intel."

I sprang forward and charged him down. We were roughly ten metres apart, and I got almost five metres before he discharged his gun.

***

As we got out of the car this time for the president to do his walkabout, the air felt different. I looked up at the sky and it was a hazy cloud partially blocking the sun.

The weather has changed. This made my heart race more than ever. *What is changing? How is this changing? Has anything else changed? What damage am I doing?*

We approached the stage one more time, with my sense of time running out.

This next time I moved even earlier, faking left as I ran at the gunman, keeping low and striking him in the waist with my shoulder; the gun going off as he fell backwards.

A spotlight above as exploded with the impact, and we crashed to the floor. The other agents were on us and grappled the gun out of his hand.

"Get out of here! Pull back! Pull back! All agents, secure POTUS and head to the Beasts, rear of stage. Repeat. Rear of stage. As soon as POTUS is secure, move out." Li and Salanski took the president either side and we moved to the car.

Once inside, Turner pulled the door closed, and as the door clicked shut, we sped away.

Li turned from his position in the front seat "Great job, Doc. I didn't spot that one coming."

Salanski slapped me on the shoulder. "Good to have you on the team."

I looked up and met McDonald's eyes. He studied me for a moment, and then held out his hand. "Thank you,

Doctor Hill. Your country, and myself all owe you a debt of gratitude."

A wave of relief washed over me. "My pleasure, sir." I sat forward and remembered my job in this operation. "Sir, are you injured at all?"

The president looked down at his torso and patted his stomach. "Nothing I haven't done to myself over the years."

We all laughed as we pulled back into Winfield House. As we entered the operations room, Agent Del Fonte came striding up to us. My gut tightened. "Mr President, sir. Are you OK? We saw what happened on the news."

McDonald put up his hands in a placating motion. "No need to panic, Gina. Doctor Hill reacted quickly and decisively and saved me from the gunman."

Li was watching the screens at the end of the room. "Do we know who he is yet?"

"Just got word from the Met Police. He was one of the security guards for President P'il Songhyon."

Salanski tensed as he heard this. "Knew we shouldn't trust him."

"Unlikely the president of Korea has anything to do with this, Agent Salanski. He was most likely a rouge agent working for the Hwarang."

"Where is he now?" I asked.

"Been taken to Paddington Green station in London. It's where they keep their terrorists. They have him and the guy that tried to grab you in the crowd during the walkabout, sir," Del Fonte said as she looked at the president. "Which I must say, sir. With respect, was a very dangerous move."

McDonald flashed his smile at her, and then turned as we were interrupted by one of the analysts. "Sirs, ma'am. Gim is broadcasting again."

"Put it up."

A video appeared on screen that showed Gim in the same location he was when he appeared on the jumbotrons outside the palace.

The same armed militia flanked him, but something was different.

Li got there first. "Different colour shirt from earlier." It was obvious when he said it.

"Sirs, ma'am," said the analyst. "It appears to be a video playing on repeat from a site on the dark web."

He brought the sound up on the video, and the room fell to a hush as Gim's voice once again filled the air.

"...comply with my demands. If you do not, I will unleash hell upon you. Im jeon mu toe!" The video ended.

"Hang on, it is about to restart," the analyst said.

A symbol of a flower and a knight on horseback appeared on screen, quickly replaced by Gim's face.

"Mr President McDonald. I address you and the entire group of nations you represent. As you have by now seen, I have seized control of the city of London. No longer will it have power, or infrastructure. I am in control. All of your cities will fall. One by one. You are nothing without your computers, your cars, and your homes that will soon die and become useless as their fuel cells run out. Your banks and your supermarkets will no longer function. You will not be able to talk on your phones, or spread your propaganda across the world. You will not be able to travel. You will not be able to go about your daily lives as you know them now. You will be reduced to a third world country in a matter of days, unless I give you back what I took today.

"As I said in my address to you today, I have a simple set of requests.

"One. NATO and the US cease all activities in North Korea. NATO and the US withdraw all troops immediately from North Korea. Two. The treaty will not be signed as planned today. Three. You, Mr President McDonald will meet with me and publicly acknowledge the Hwarang as a political group and member of the North Korean assembly. The Flowering Knights will rise up and take their rightful place at the set of the world!"

Gim leaned into the camera as he spoke his final lines. "To make sure you are clear that I am serious in my demands, Mr President McDonald, I have put a timer on the site you are viewing this video on. It is set for noon today in

UK time. If you do not comply by then, there will be consequences. If you try and stop me, there will be a price to pay. You have until the timer runs out to comply with my demands. If you do not, I will unleash hell upon you. Im jeon mu toe!"

"That's it," the analyst said. "It just loops back around from here."

I was stunned for a moment. *I have no idea how to stop this guy. No one does.*

"Where is this timer?" Del Fonte demanded.

"Here, ma'am." The analyst brought up the site. It was a web page that had the video they had just seen in the centre, and a large digital clock counting down to noon at the top.

I looked at my watch to double check. It was only eight minutes to noon. Eight minutes to go.

"What does he mean by 'unleash hell'? What could he be capable of doing next?" McDonald asked.

"We know he has taken control of London infrastructure, sir," Del Fonte said.

"Show me."

The analyst brought up surveillance footage of London. He zoomed in and out of various locations across the capital.

"If you take a look, you can see that there is a blackout right across the city."

Sure enough, all offices, shops and billboards were completely dark. The streets were filled with people pouring out of buildings, all looking around at each other, and the area surrounding them.

"What about that one – still has the lights on," Li pointed out.

"Yes, sir. One of the hospitals. St Thomas', sir. They will have a backup generator in the basement somewhere in case of this situation."

"And how long will that last for?"

"Batteries are charged off the grid, so roughly twenty-four hours or there about."

"I can still see cars moving. Guess they will run out at some point."

"Yes, most modern cars can last for up to five hundred miles on a full charge, but need plugging in soon."

"So he's got us by the short and curlies then."

"Can we undo the hack?" McDonald asked.

"Most likely, sir," the analyst said. "We are working with UK authorities now to try and undo it. But there is not much time. And it would be useful to know where they are doing it from."

"Could be anywhere in the world."

"Yes, sir, but you would need to be on the network to do some of this. Have to be connected to the hard lines of London's infrastructure."

"Good, well that narrows it down to a few million people."

"Sirs, ma'am. We are getting reports from London authorities. Something is happening over at Battersea."

"Show me."

He brought up a live picture of Battersea Power Station. An historic building built in the 1930s as a coal burning power station; it was decommissioned in 1975, and had changed hands with various commercial operations until 2035, when the UK government bought it back, and converted it to a nuclear power plant in 2042.

There was much controversy surrounding its build. Many lobbyists didn't want a nuclear power plant in the heart of the city, but government pressure won out in the end, and the first mid-city plant was built in the UK.

Now that the plant was on screen, my heart sank at the thought of what could happen next.

"Is that… the power plant?" McDonald asked, already knowing the answer.

"Yes, sir. London authorities have already ordered its evacuation."

Fat lot of good that would do. I thought. You need to get to the next country over to be safe.

"Look!" Li had jumped in the air and was waving at the screen.

At first, I couldn't make out what I was seeing, but then I realised it was smoke pouring out of the side of the building.

Was it smoke, or steam? I couldn't tell. Could be either. But whatever it was, it was growing in density.

"Message coming in across the mobile network, sirs, ma'am," the analyst said.

Mobile phones chimed and bleeped across the room. I feared it was Li again. But no, this time the message was even more stark.

Del Fonte had hers out and was reading out the message. "From the HM Government and the Mayor of London: A major incident has been declared at the Nuclear Power Plant at Battersea. All residents of the greater London area are strongly advised to stay in their homes and close all windows and doors until you receive further instructions. Emergency services are on the scene and are dealing with the incident."

She put her phone away and turned to the room. "OK, everybody evac the building. Mr President, sir, we need to get you as far from here as possible. Li, organise your team and prepare Marine One for immediate departure. Everyone else, close down, pack up and head North. We will arrange for evac out of the country as soon as possible."

I opened my mouth, then closed it again. Li was already assigning agents to the chopper. Alongside myself, Li and Salanski were Turner, Stephens and a small handful of advisers. Del Fonte was to remain in London.

"Agent Li. May I have a word?" I tentatively approached my superior.

"Doctor?"

"Is Marine One wise, sir? There is a chance we could be shot down."

Li was having roughly three conversations at the same time with various agents and officials.

"Always that risk, Agent Hill. Marine One is well equipped to deal with that eventuality."

"Yes, but sir—"

Li stopped and turned to face me.

"What would you have me do, Doctor? You saw the same broadcast I did. The roads are already jammed. I need to get the president as far from here as I possibly can in the shortest space of time."

He looked at me for a beat, and then carried on organising.

We were all walking with the president across the lawn toward the helicopter, rotors already spinning up when we heard the first explosion.

It was a dull *whump* from the distance. We all stopped and looked skyward. A plume of smoke was seen drifting up into the skyline. At the same moment, I swear I felt the ground shake. It was as though I was standing on a rug and someone at the other end of the room flicked it to send a wave like ripple down the ground toward me.

Others must have felt it too, as we all, including the president, momentarily stopped and put their hands out, as if to find their balance.

We looked at each other with wide eyes.

"We need to go *now*!"

We rushed up the steps and buckled ourselves in as we left the lawn of Winfield House.

As soon as we rose up to cruising altitude, we banked left and headed west. We had to take a wide route around London so to not get too close to Battersea. As we turned, we had a clear view across the capital out of the portside window.

And there it was. The iconic building I had seen as a college student on the *Pink Floyd* album cover. The one with a floating balloon pig over the top. *Pig*? Really? Was this just a coincidence, or where they tipping us off? Or just rubbing our faces in it?

Whichever it was, the site that greeted us had the whole group of us gawping out of the window in disbelief.

Battersea Nuclear Power Station was ablaze.

The roof was burning. But it wasn't like any other fire I had seen. It was as close to a bright white glow in the centre as could be possible.

The surrounding edges changed to a yellow glow. But glow didn't cover it. It was a fierce, angry looking sight. The inferno was billowing a thick, black smoke. So dark and heavy that it didn't billow in the wind like normal smoke would. It looked heavier, like it had real substance to it.

It looked like hell on Earth. Gim was correct in what he promised.

I looked over at Li, Turner and Salanski and they all were still staring, mouths open. McDonald was quiet. I thought I caught him wiping his eye before he turned to Li. "Tell the pilot to get us to Paris as fast as we can."

"Sir. Yes, sir. Where in Paris in particular, sir?"

"The embassy there. We need to be secure. And we need to be as far from *that* as we can get on a tank of fuel."

Li nodded and left his seat.

I was running through all of the possible ways I could intervene, and who I could tell who wouldn't just put me in a mental asylum and throw away the key.

We banked again and levelled off to head out of the city, but as we did, we slowed down and hovered over the river.

At that moment the pilot came over the intercom. "Mr President, sir. I'm afraid we will not be able to leave British airspace." Li opened the door to the cockpit so we could all see him.

"What do you mean, pilot?" demanded McDonald.

"I mean, sir, that the ionisation from the blast down there had knocked out our primary fuel cells. Our reserve batteries will only keep us airborne for another fifteen minutes."

McDonald stood up from his seat and paced in the small cabin. "Options?"

"We can get as far as the outer edges of London and recharge."

"How long to recharge?"

"About an hour, but could only get another fifty miles on these cells. Not enough to get away fast enough."

"What about alternative aircraft?"

"We can have another copter brought over, but wouldn't reach us until tomorrow. And if we use anything other than our own; would be playing into the terrorists' hands."

Salanski ran his hands through his hair. "We may not have any other choice. That or be blown to pieces by a meltdown."

"Come on, you saw what happened to that news copter. Gim can't wait for us to switch to a non-secure vehicle."

McDonald was pacing as the others argued. "Any bunkers we can use? London must have them."

Li looked up from his laptop that he was using to search for a way out. "Yes. Downing Street will have them. Excellent idea, Mr President."

The president nodded. "OK, radio into the prime minister. Tell him we are coming in. Pilot, set a course."

The pilot turned and headed back to central London, as I sat and wondered how much darker this day could get.

Eight

The fallout shelter under Number 10 Downing Street was not just under the building itself. It stretched for miles in a network of tunnels between where we were and the Houses of Parliament.

What started as a fallout shelter in the last century, has now become a nerve centre of operations, with office, retail and sleeping quarters for more than two thousand staff and VIPs on any given working day.

When they said fallout shelter, I conjured up an image of cold grey concrete walls, a few bulbs swinging from wires in the ceiling, and cold steel bunk beds with brown itchy blankets where people ate out of small ration tins, and dreamt of home.

Maybe there would be a man in the corner on a desk with a pair of headphones on, tapping out a Morse code message to the outside world.

So I was more than taken aback when we walked down a plush carpeted stairway to a hotel reception. There was a concierge, maids moving back and forth and signs that pointed to *gym*, *pool*, *cinema* and *restaurant*.

We checked in at the desk, where we were asked "Will you be requiring dinner reservations this evening?"

"Well, er, yes please." I exchanged a look with Salanski and Li, who leaned over to my ear.

"Hey, if this is the end of the world, I'm all in."

We were shown to our rooms, my roommate was Salanski. We dumped our stuff and kicked back on our single beds, ate the complimentary chocolates and switched on the TV. We watched the news for a while. The rolling footage showed me tackling the gunman, and Gim's face looming over Buckingham Palace.

"OK, I need some time out," said Salanski as he brought up the in-house movie selection.

I didn't complain. I needed some R&R too.

Most of our team had been relocated, us just making the trip back without incident before power in our helicopter ran out.

It was busy in there with the British party as well as the US, and some of the NATO guests that made it down in time. I spent the night in our room with Salanski, who, thankfully, was not a snorer. Less could be said for the room next door, whose Belgium dignitaries sounded like they were trying to boar their way out; the rumbling noise was so loud.

The next morning, we went down for breakfast, and met the rest of the team in the restaurant.

I felt thankful for being here in this moment, with so many people in a dire situation outside. I felt for the families that have already lost their lives, or in danger of it, as London was under heavy evacuation, and the roads and transport networks were jammed with people in a state of panic trying to flee with their loved ones.

We were watching the morning news feed in the restaurant and it was harrowing.

The BBC had sent a drone in to capture images of the streets surrounding Battersea, and nearby Victoria and Parliament Square.

We followed the camera as it flew up and over iconic landmarks such as Tower Bridge, and followed the river towards Whitehall.

From there it swept down along the embankment, and along and up until it reached Westminster Bridge.

The scene was like something out of a movie. Vehicles were abandoned on the streets, and there was no movement.

As the camera zoomed in, we could see people still in their cars. But they were badly blistered. Their faces had been burned to a red and black, and all were lifeless. At the moment the image focussed in, it cut away abruptly to a shocked reporter.

"I'm sorry if you saw some scenes that you may have found distressing. We are seeing this for the first time as you are." The anchor touched his ear. "OK, I think we can go back to the scenes in London now."

The drone image reappeared and this time we were heading down Victoria Street towards Battersea.

"What is that? Snow?" asked Del Forte who was sat beside me.

Thick flakes were falling over the capital, and leaving a blanket over everything. It wasn't cold outside, certainly not cold enough to snow.

"Ash," said one of the UK dignitaries, sitting opposite me. "Thick ash. From the meltdown."

"Oh my." Gina had her hand up to her mouth.

I sat as helpless as any one of us were at that moment. I needed to do something, or tell someone. But I could only think of one person who would possibly believe me. "Ma'am?"

Del Forte was still watching, a tear rolled down her check.

I cleared my throat. "Ma'am?"

"Sorry, Doctor, what is it?" She snapped out of her thoughts.

"Can we talk in private?"

We were interrupted by noise coming from the adjacent room.

As we arrived, most of the people in the bunker were crammed into the war room. Salanski and Li were already there, flanking the president, the first lady and the vice president, Davis Dawson.

As soon as McDonald saw us, he beckoned us over to him and his wife. He extended his hand as we approached, grabbing it firmly and cupping the other over the top as he looked me in the eye. "I felt I never fully said thank you for what you did yesterday, Agent Hill."

I felt a lump form in the back of my throat. "All part of my duty, Mr President, sir."

He smiled and patted me on the shoulder. "Nevertheless, your actions saved my life, and I shall be forever indebted to you."

The First Lady Sally McDonald – or Sallymac as the press called her, mouthed a thank you to me, as her eyes glistened.

Gina broke the silence. "What's happening?" Salanski was standing the other side of her.

"British intelligence has been tracking movement in and out of the UK, and a source tipped them off on a possible sighting of Gim. They are getting a team ready to go in now."

I looked up at the screen and could see a grainy image of the outside of a building and what looked like an old stone wall.

There was audio coming over in, but it was faint. "Red Spear team in position."

The room was silent. Salanski leaned over to my ear. "Operation underway. They think he is in this safe house. An undercover agent spotted him going in late last night. Travelled down from the north."

I looked at the image as it rose up, and moved up and down as it went six feet along the ground and sunk back down.

"Head cam of the squadron leader. About to storm the place. Man, I wish I was there to get that son of a bitch."

I could see the edge of the building; a field and tractor were visible to the periphery of the shot.

"Where is this?" I asked.

"About twenty miles south east of Calais, northern France, near the border with Brussels. They think he was in London yesterday, and fled south just before they blew the power station."

My mind searched for the images I had seen of Gim. "The countdown was a recording."

"Say again?"

"When Gim was seen at Buckingham Palace, it was live. The countdown on the site afterward was a recording."

"So he could get out before the explosion. Damn. He must have been in London. But…" Salanski rubbed his temples. "Why be here at all? Could have been anywhere in the world."

I thought for a moment. "Of course. Someone needs to be physically connected to the power station to hack it. The security on those things must be extreme."

"But why him? Could have sent anyone to do it?"

"Wants to oversee it personally. Biggest night of his life. Didn't want someone else to mess it…" I stopped dead in my tracks.

"What is it?" Salanski was looking at me, waiting for my response.

"He was at the power station. Or at least near it."

"Yeah, isn't that what I just said?"

I looked at the screen in front of me as the squadron made their advance. "Red Spear One moving in."

Dawson leaned into the president. "Sir, we should take Gim alive. The intel could be invaluable."

The commander in the control room heard the comment. "Take him alive if at all possible. Use deadly force if not."

The room was still.

The soldier stood up and jogged along to the edge of the wall where he squatted. He waved his hand near his visor, stood and moved around the corner to the entrance. He passed the door, turned and stood flat against the wall; the other four members of his team in front of him.

His hand gestured twice, and the soldier in front of him put a hand to the door handle. He removed his hand and shook his head.

The soldier took a step back and shot the lock and moved rapidly to position himself in front of the squadron leader, turned sideways at the entrance.

After a beat, they moved in. They all rushed in the door and moved to a flanking position. Inside was a sparse room with a wooden table to the side, and an old couch in the opposite corner. Silence permeated the operations room.

A doorway lay ahead, and the team approached stealthily. I could see that the building was in disrepair, with paper peeling off the walls, and gaps in the floorboards where, presumable, water leaking form above had caused it to rot through.

They covered the twelve feet across the space, but stopped short of crossing the threshold. The leader crouched down and produced a spray can which he used to spray a white smoke toward the ground. A fine wire running taught at ankle level across the doorway glistened in the haze. The team leader stood and stepped over it, as the rest followed suit.

The doorway led to a short corridor, with a staircase to the left, and another room ahead.

The team moved and checked the room beyond, which was empty. They turned to face the stairway, as something moved into shot. "Grenade!" was shouted over the radio. The image dropped to the floor and went dark for a moment, then a loud bag was heard. The image jumped back up and looked around. Dust and debris covered the room, and the squadron got back to their feet.

A gunman appeared at the foot of the stairs and fired at the troops. The crack of gunfire erupted as two more appeared on the stairwell. The troops fired back, and wood splinters flew off the banisters as all three men fell.

"Red Spear One move forward." The team stepped over the bodies of the fallen gunmen, and ascended the staircase, again stopping short of the top.

The camera creeped up, inch by inch, to reveal the upper floor. Even I could see the trip wire this time, and so had the soldiers. But beyond the wire was an open plan room with more broken wooden floorboards. There was only one piece of furniture in the corner; a mattress on the floor. And on it was a man and a woman. The face was unmistakable.

Gim.

He was wearing a simple cream coloured shirt, and black combat trousers, and in his hand, he held up a short stick with a button. His thumb was pressed down on it, the knuckles visibly white.

He grinned as he spoke. "Can you hear me out there, McDonald? Are you watching this?"

He stood and held the stick out in front of him. "Did they tell you to bring me in alive? How well do you think this will go?"

"Team retreat to outside, repeat, retreat to outside."

The camera whirled around as the sound of Gim laughing could be heard. The final voice on the transmission was Gim's "Remember the Lynx! Im jeon mu toe!"

The screen changed to static.

McDonald held his hand to his mouth. "Commander?"

The man at the radio punched buttons on his keyboard. "Red Spear One come in, repeat, Red Spear One, report."

I grabbed Gina by the arm. "We need to talk. Now."

She was shaking, but nodded as she headed for the door; almost running as tears rolled down her cheeks.

We made our way to a small ante room and sat at a table. She looked at me with red eyes and shook her head. "Those soldiers, did we just watch…" She trailed off before she could say it.

I swallowed hard and tried to gather my thoughts. "Ma'am, I know a way to stop all of this. I think I am in a position to be able to stop Gim."

Del Forte leaned in. "Did you not see what just happened? He just blew himself to kingdom come!"

"I know, but his… his cell will still be active. This isn't over. But what if I told you I could reverse everything that had happened over the last day."

She narrowed her eyes as she sized me up. "This is not the time for jokes, Doctor Hill. People have died."

"Yes, I know, but please, humour me for a second. I realise this is going to sound crazy. But we won't have much time."

Gina laughed. "Right now, with us not being able to leave to get to the surface until the radiation is safe, we have a lot of time, Doctor Hill." She sighed and let her shoulders drop. She raised her palms up to the ceiling. "But I'm all ears."

Here we go with the crazy talk. I breathed in, and breathed out, collecting my thoughts. "I don't know how this is happening, but I have been reliving the same day, the last twenty-four hours in fact, over and over again."

She sighed and looked at the floor, shaking her head slowly.

"I'm telling you the truth. I have been living the same day over and over. I don't know how, or why it is happening, but it is. I can go back to just before the explosion and stop it, if I knew when and where to go."

She reached out and placed her hand on mine. It was soft and tender. "Doctor Hill, Gibson. We have all been under a lot of stress today, it's OK to feel confused and—"

"I'm telling you the truth!" I slam my fist on the table.

Del Forte pulled back and put her hands up. "OK, I'm going to leave now. I think we should all take a break. If you still think like this in the morning, I'm going to recommend you talk to Doctor Davis."

"I don't need a physiatrist!" I was getting louder as I spoke. "I'm telling you the truth!"

"Oh, that you can relive the same day over and over. Stop wasting my time. Good day, Doctor Hill."

She turned to leave the room. "No, wait. You said once before that there was a soldier in Korea. What was his name? Hart. That was it, a soldier named Hart. He kept having visions, or saying he could predict the future."

Del Forte had her hand on the door handle but turned back to face me. I moved close to her, our faces inches from each other. I tried to moderate my voice to calm her down.

"Hart was crazy. He was court martialled. Got off on an insanity plea. He is not worth getting involved with."

"Just… just tell me about him," I ask.

She let go of the door handle and her shoulders dropped. I could see she was angry and tired, the streaks of tears still visible on her cheeks, but I knew she could help, if I could convince her.

"OK, I'll tell you about him. But after that; I want you to go and see Doctor Davis. Just to have a chat. If fact, I'm going to recommend we all do." She paused for a moment. "OK, so he was a soldier. One of the best we had. No. *The* best we had. Had a sixth sense when it came to danger. Would seem to know when things were coming before we all did. The only reason we all got out alive."

"Go on," I said.

"But he went crazy. Said that he could see visions of the future and know when things were coming. But then he went really very crazy indeed. Said that if he didn't stop, the world would end. Proper crazy stuff. Starting saying he was a martyr, that he could control the future. That's when he was arrested."

"Why? Why was he arrested?"

Gina sighed again. "He knew things he couldn't have possibly have known unless he was deep inside the enemy's intelligence operations." Her voice was getting louder again. "And if you tell me you can see the future too…"

I put a hand on her arm. "Gina." She looked up at me. "I promise you, I am not crazy, but something is happening, and I need help."

"OK," she said breathing out with pursed lips. "I like you, Doctor. I had you down as one of the good guys. What can I possibly do?"

I thought for a moment, then I had it. "I need you to tell me something."

"What do you mean?"

"Tell me something I could not possibly know, and couldn't find out on social media or online or talking to any friends."

"What is this, Gibson? I'm tired. We all are." She turned to leave.

"Just. Just trust me. Do this and it will be the end of this."

She sighed and thought. "OK, I'll play along. What the hell. But you are going straight to Doctor Davis."

A moment passed between us before she spoke again.

"Los Pollitos."

"What is that?"

"It's a nursery rhyme my mother used to sing to me when she was pregnant with my brother."

"Thank you."

"Can you promise me that you will get help if you need it?" She said this earnestly, a sincere look of concern in her eyes.

I paused for a moment. "I think I already have." I grabbed the gun in the holster on her side, and before she could stop me, sent myself back to the Beast.

Nine

Once I woke, I instantly 'freaked out', knowing that the same would happen as before; Salanski would take me out of the car and we would walk back to Winfield House. Instead, this time, I jogged back. Salanski was doing his best to keep up "Doc? Doc, you suddenly feeling better?"

I ignored his protests and pushed into a sprint, heart about to explode, but every minute counted. Plus, for the first time in I don't know how long, I felt good.

When we arrived at Winfield House, Gina was already there as the last time. She saw us enter the room, but before she could speak, I went straight up to her "I need to talk to you in private." I walked her out of the operations room and down the corridor to a small meeting space.

"Doctor, are you—"

"Yes, I'm OK. I need your help, and there is not much time."

"Sure, Gibs—"

"Remember Hart? David Hart? You all thought he had gone crazy in Korea."

Her expression hardened. "Gibson, what are you saying?"

"He wasn't crazy. I think whatever happened to him is happening to me. In fact, we have had this conversation before."

"Jeez, you need to find hel—"

"You are my help, I'm not crazy, we had this conversation in Downing Street—"

"Downing Street? Doctor, what do you mean Downing Street? We never went there?"

"Yes, we spoke earlier, I mean we will speak there. OK, I asked you to tell me something I couldn't know. You told me you mother used to sing a Spanish song to you as a little girl: Los Pollitos."

"How…?" Her eyes were glistening.

"I told you. I am reliving the same day; today, over and over again. In a few minutes Gim is going to hack into London's infrastructure and first bring down a news helicopter onto the roof of Buckingham Palace, and then send Battersea Power Station into meltdown. I'm not the enemy, I haven't got info from the Koreans, I have lived this already, and I'm telling you—"

We were interrupted by an analyst. "Ma'am, something bad is happening, Gim has—"

"Hacked us?" Gina looked at me, questioning.

"Yes, ma'am, how did you know?"

"Leave us for a moment, I will be there in one minute." She turned to me. "You have thirty seconds to convince me." She held her finger up to stop me speaking. "And not just a nursery rhyme."

I thought for a moment. "Think of a number. A number that is important to you."

"Seriously, you will have to do better than that."

"Just trust me. Give me a number."

"Fine. Seven."

I lunged for her gun once more.

Ten

"…told me you mother used to sing a Spanish song to you as a little girl; Los Pollitos."

"How…?"

"In about twenty seconds, an analyst is going to come into this room to tell you that we have been hacked. Think of a number."

"What… what?"

"Quickly – think of a number that is important to you, but don't tell me. Seven. Right?"

"OK, this is some magic trick. What am I holding behind my back?"

Damn. Back in the Beast.

"…In about twenty seconds, an analyst is going to come into this room to tell you that we have been hacked. Think of a number that is important to you."

"Wha—"

"Seven. The number of times you applied to the Service before they accepted you and took you seriously. Right now, you are undoing your watch and dropping it into your hand."

She opened her mouth, but no sound came out.

"An analyst is about to walk in to tell you Gim has hacked London. Tell him you will be there in one minute."

She turned just as the analyst was walking in.

"Ma'am, something bad is happening, Gim has—"

"Hacked us? I'll be there in a minute."

She turned back to me and tried to gather her thoughts. "Oooh, OK, OK," She breathed out hard to the floor, "This is weird. How are you—"

I was running out of patience. "We have no time left, we need to find out where Gim is hiding, so I can get to him on the next loop. It's the only way. Get McDonald out of there now, and we need to evacuate everyone from London, taking Marine One on a wide arc to the west, as I think there are insurgents with a surface to air launcher directly to the south."

She shook her head to clear it. "OK. I'll believe you. For now. But this is freaking me out. Hart was…" She trailed off.

I put my hands on her shoulders to focus her. "Del Fonte. Gina. We have no time."

"Yes, yes of course." She shook herself and cleared her throat.

I could see that I had caught her off guard this time. She was moving from foot to foot, starting to move towards the door, then changing her mind and stepping back.

I had made her nervous and indecisive.

"OK," she said after a moment, "follow me."

We left and headed back to the operations room. Gim was already on screen. Gina was direct and authoritative. "OK everyone, instruct all agents to pull back. Bring McDonald back here ASAP."

People put fingers to headsets. There was a flurry of switching channels, and "Come in" for around thirty seconds, those thirty seconds which felt like an hour as we couldn't get hold of our guys in the field fast enough.

"Ma'am. I'm afraid we have lost all comms. No contact."

"Shit. Any way to get hold of them?"

I thought for a moment. "Phones are still operational." I turned to whisper to Gina. "Gim dials everyone in the area as a stunt."

"Get Li or Stephens on the phone. Tell them to pull back now."

An analyst was dialling from a mobile phone on his desk. One of the secure line networks that are given out to all agents in the field, should such this situation arise.

I watched on screen as the agents stood without reaching for their handsets. Then I saw Stephens move up the rear stirs, phone in hand.

My blood pressure dropped a few millibars.

"Also see the guard, second from the left of P'il Songhyon? He is a shooter. Check him for a mask like the ones in the crowd."

Gina was talking on the phone to Stephens, who I could see on screen creeping up behind the guard. He placed a hand on his shoulder. The guard span round and pulled his gun, but Stephens was too quick. He had disarmed him, and got him on the floor just as Li rushed over.

I could hear exited voices of the otherwise calm reporters on the news as they were capturing something other than just a few boring speeches, read out my men in grey suits.

You want something to report on, I thought. *Just wait a beat*.

Other agents grabbed McDonald and pulled him away as the camera panned in on the grappling men on the floor. Li produced a pig mask, and held it aloft for all to see.

Cheers erupted from the operations room. Gina fist pumped the air and we high-fived. The sense of relief was immeasurable. *Had we done it?* It all felt too easy.

I watched as the agents bundled McDonald off the stage, and into the cars. The news cameras followed the convoy as they and their police escorts pulled out of Buckingham Palace at speed; motorcycle outriders aggressively clearing a path as they wound their way back towards home base. Back to Winfield House.

As a contemplated this though, and, to be honest, took a few moments to compose myself, Gina whispered in my ear. "Now what happens?"

At that moment, as if to answer her question, Gim appeared on screen. "This is to all who listen. McDonald has retreated. I asked for an audience, and he has denied me. To die in battle is an honour. To retreat, a disgrace! Im jeon mu toe! All of you will suffer the consequences for his cowardice!"

Gina looked at me "What now?"

Gim's face had disappeared from the screen. Cries of *Aelililililil* could be heard over the crowd.

"I don't know. This has never happened before."

We felt the explosion before we heard it.

Eleven

Once I found Gina, and had my patter of convincing her down to thirty seconds, we decided to head off Gim, or his cell at Battersea ourselves.

We had tried calling ahead, we spoke to several people at the power station, but they just thought we were hoaxing them. So, the only option we had left was to get down there.

This was going to be no mean feat, as we had little time to get through the busy London traffic, and even less time to get to where we needed to be and stop things.

This was looking like more and more an impossible task. We were being thwarted at every turn, and every time we seemed to get somewhere, we were put several paces back.

I was starting to get tired. Not physically. I had long since realised that my physical state reset with each jump back, so I was not diminishing in that respect, nor did I think I would age. But who knew? Ageing is such a slow process that you can normally only see it happen when you look back at old photos of yourself, which is what I had done a couple of times. I took a few pics just kicking around London in the few days before, and every so often had pulled out the image and compared it to myself in the bathroom mirror at Winfield House.

I could see any change. But it is, as I said, a slow process. After a few hundred resets back to the Beast, then maybe I might see the odd grey hair creeping in.

Maybe one day my colleagues would all get the shock of their lives when an old man appears in the rear seats next to them, ranting about a bomb and a shooter.

No, it was mentally that I was feeling tired. My mind was stressed, just the weight of the world bearing down on me like an anvil, turning the screw with every failed attempt, every rests, and every time I saw those images of those people. The ones in the cars in particular. The families that had been burned beyond all recognition by radiation.

And for what? To make a government sit up and take you seriously? Who could do that? Who thinks like that? Who spends their life pouring energy into hating, into exacting revenge, making sure people know that you were in the right, and that your point of few matters, even if the reason for your opinion has been lost to time?

It's petty. It's petulant, like a small child gets. It's the kid who won't play nicely with others and sits on the bench at playtime with their arms folded and bottom lip jutting out.

It's insecure. That's what it is. Most people are reasonable, aren't they? Can we just sit and have an adult conversation? No. Obviously not. I forgot about the overriding fact here.

Power.

Power changed people from reasonable beings to blood thirsty sociopaths in the flick of an election ballot, or the cocking of a gun.

And there was one more thing that comes into play. More powerful that any weapon, more dangerous than any bomb; ladies and gentlemen (drum roll please) – the male ego. Boom. There. I said it. Can't be seen to back down now, can we, boys? Your fragile psyche can't handle saying the words 'I was wrong', it just doesn't look good in front of the mirror. Those deep dark insecurities could possibly be harmed by anything other than the image of you being absolutely all knowledgeable and all powerful. So you won't back down. Ever. Never ever. It hurts your feelings too much.

Those are the people in power. Those are the ones in control.

I let out yet another sigh. Was I on a losing battle?

No. I refuse to believe that. I refuse to believe that I can't effect a change.

But sometimes you just want to stop the world and get off, right?

We made our escape out of the side entrance of Winfield House, via the kitchen (I snagged a croissant on the way; hey, why not?).

"Hey, come on." Gina looked impatient. I hadn't realised that I had stopped walking and was just munching down the last of my pastry. "There's time for that later."

Ain't that the truth.

We got out onto the street and looked around. "There." Gina pointed a rank of cars for hire, lined up on the street a few hundred yards from us. We approached the kiosk next to the first little city car and I pulled out my credit card.

It took us five agonising minutes to pay for it and unlock the car. It was one of those ones that you had to register an account before it would let you take it. *Mental note to self. Create an account next time.* We pulled out of the bay, pointed the car south west, and headed straight to Battersea.

The roads were jammed on the way towards the power plant, and the sat nav I had programmed in told us it would take twenty-three minutes to get there. We had moved just over a mile in the last ten.

"This isn't the daring rescue operation I had planned." Gina puffed out her cheeks and blew.

We tried taking a detour and made it as far as Hyde Park before we heard the explosion.

***

The next time I set a different route to take us away from the traffic, and we got to within a quarter of a mile of Battersea before I was sent back to the Beast.

***

The next time we drove like crazies, mounting the curbs and sending people screaming for cover. We got almost ten minutes away that time.

***

We were in the front seat of the car for the fourth time and still making no better progress. This time hitting almost ninety down the narrow streets of London. "We need something else," I said as we ground to a halt once again.

"What did you have in mind?"

***

Outside Winfield House I ran past the row of cars, and out onto Park Road. Gina was doing well to catchup. He had taken off her business-like shoes and was carrying them as she jogged behind me barefoot. "What are you looking for?"

I spotted what I needed as it swung into view. "Gina. Your gun." I held out my hand as she unholstered her weapon.

I stepped out in front of the rider and aimed the pistol at him. He initially tried to swerve and avoid me, but I let off a round and chipped a small hole in the asphalt in from of him.

He screeched to a halt with his hands in the air.

"I need your bike. Get off." I said it with the gun pointed at his head in one hand, and my Service badge held up in the other. The man dismounted and stood away with his hands in the air as I jumped on with Gina climbing on behind me.

I squeezed the throttle back and surged forward as Gina's arms wrapped tightly around my waist.

We sailed through the traffic, Gina leaning intuitively with me as we swung left and right around cars and busses as we carved a route south.

We arrived at Battersea with six minutes to spare.

Twelve

We arrived at the power station to find it had a visitors' centre at the front, with a line of tourists queuing to get in.

The line reached a ticket booth, and to the side, a set of turnstiles provided the gate to let people through, once the admission price had been paid.

The glass box bolted onto the front of the building served as an atrium, with tourists shaking off the rain as the stepped inside, the floor a muddy slippery mess.

The entrance hall was bustling with activity. I tour guide was introducing herself to a group of twenty or so Americans, and next to them a translator was talking to a small Japanese delegation, all of the taking pictures of everything and anything.

There was a side door where the security guards were posted, watching the queue as is slowly filed in. We approached the guards and flashed our badges. They looked as though we had awakened them, and they weren't sure where they were.

"Secret service. We need to talk to your head of security." They looked at us, then looked at each other, and realised this was way above their pay grade, and so opened the door.

We ran past the groups and the queue of people waiting and straight up to the reception desk, flashing our badges as we went.

We reached the reception desk, where the head of security was standing.

The head of security on the desk was a middle-aged man with neatly trimmed sideburns, beer belly and an air of arrogance that comes with someone who has been given a position of authority, and liked to abuse it.

He stiffened and moved around the desk to intercept us as we approached.

"You can't come in here. Authorised personnel only." He waved his hand at us in a shooing motion.

"US Secret Service, sir. We have reason to believe that terrorists are about to bring down this power plant. You need to shut down all operations and evacuate immediately."

The guard clearly didn't like being told what to do. He was in a position of power, but clearly inept at it, as any security operation would recognise the service and respect them, and want to work with them. This was a man who clearly spent his life covering his ass; usually covering up his own shortcomings.

People who are competent and confident in what they do usually have no problem in bowing to superior knowledge, in the hope they can learn something.

He puffed out his chest and rocked back on his heals. "Battersea is not under any control of terrorists; we have the highest level of—"

He was interrupted by a scream from the woman on the desk, and the receptionist put her hand to her mouth and gasped. She was watching the news on her phone under the desk, and I knew what she had seen before she said it. "They just crashed a helicopter onto the palace roof!" Tears were running down her face.

The news had quickly spread as the line of tourists outside. Panic was beginning to set in.

I looked the security guard dead in the eye, inches from his face. "That was the work of the Korean terrorist known as Gim. We are here because our intelligence tells us that in exactly two minutes from now, they will hack into the infrastructure of this power plant and cause a nuclear explosion; the likes that have not been seen for decades. Now, I am telling you this only because you are standing between us and the ability to stop this from happening. I am doing this out of professional courtesy, but I have a job to do I have to prevent a major incident that will cost thousands, if not tens or hundreds of thousands of lives. So, what would you like me to tell the president? I can either tell him that you were the one who helped us defeat one of the biggest terrorist attacks on British soil this century, or I can tell him that you were part of the problem. And believe me, you don't want the US government believing you are part of the problem."

A bead of sweat broke across the man's brow. He flapped from left to right before going over to the desk. He picked up the phone and dialled. "Yes, this is front desk security… yes, it's Colin... yes, it is important this time... no, no, no… yes, yes, yes, just listen – I have the US Secret Service here, and they say we are in danger of—"

He was cut off by a siren from deep within the building. The lights in the foyer dimmed as the staff all looked up in shock.

People started looking up and around for the where the noise was coming from, but stayed rooted to the spot, all looking over to us for direction.

One tourist shouted over. "What does the noise mean?"

Our inept security guard remembered his position and sprang into life. "Evacuate! Everybody Evacuate!"

A few people started to move toward the doors, but most ignored him and carried on looking around for the source of the alarm.

The lights flickered, and then grew brighter, bulbs popping under the pressure. The receptionist stood and addressed the people nearby. "Can I have your attention, please. This is an emergency alarm. For your own safety, can you all exit the building by the main entrance, please leave as quickly as you can." The throng moved rapidly to the exit, as a low groan came from nearby. A noise that set the primal fear of us all on high alert.

A fierce shaking of the floor shattered the windows of the foyer, and as we ran for the doors, a sound so deafening it pushed us forward as it came from behind us, and blurred the air around us with heat.

The sensation was a warm liquid washing around me from behind, and a searing pain ripping through my body as the force of the shockwave tore at my skin, and irradiated my bones.

I felt like something had passed into me, and through me, tugging at my very core, and changing everything about me.

I managed to stumble forward, and could see the outside world just beyond my grasp.

A loud crack appeared in the ceiling above, and chunks of plaster fell to the ground, smashing onto the floor like thunder.

A second rumble started, like a storm in the distance, but growing in in tensity within seconds. The last thing I saw was a white-hot ball of fire coming at me from somewhere deep in the bowels of the power plant.

I was back in the rear seat of the Beast.

Thirteen

Am I going crazy? Is this all some elaborate practical joke? Am I part of some crazy science experiment?

I had tried everything. I had gotten straight out of the Beast and hijacked a motorbike and made it to Battersea as fast as I could. My record was six and a half minutes. Sounds fast, but once you learn every move of every car on the road you can sail through.

It became like a video game. You learn how to defeat the level. Meet the boss. Except this boss is unbeatable. Unless you pay for an upgrade. In-app purchases. That's where they get you. Except this time, I don't have access to the store. I don't have available credit. Game over, my friend; time to play something else.

I had got as far as the power station with twenty-five minutes to spare. I even went in on the bike – drove the thing right into the foyer and down the stairs to the start of the control rooms. Colin the potbellied security guard shouting as he failed to keep up.

I tried holding the technicians at gunpoint and ordering them to shut it down, but it had no effect. It was being overridden remotely, and the control rods are ejected from the core by someone else.

Even when I got the technicians on my side, and watched them do everything in their power to try and stop it, the wheels were already on motion. Control had already been seized. We were already barbecued.

I know I should be trying. Continuing to crack the problem and save the day.

But I am not there. I'm in a country pub in the far south west of England, in the Cornish town of Fowey overlooking the bay.

And I've given up.

I hijacked the same bike as before, but his time rode it away from London and kept going as far as the fuel cells would take me.

Why did I do this? Honestly? I have had enough. I have lost count of how many times I have relived this day, and failed to stop this from happening. So I made a decision to get out.

I don't know where I go from here, but it will have to be as far from the agents as possible. Perhaps even with a new name; a new identity.

As far as I see it, the only route out for me now is to disappear. Go off grid.

I will, in time, have to figure out how to stop myself being thrown back in time, and starting again, back in the rear seat of that armoured car. But for now, all I need to do is stay alive, and keep running.

Me and my new bike had arrived a picturesque part of the country. I was looking out to the bay where pleasure boats scooted about the water, some heading out to sea, others inland, where a small fishing community resided and went about their day with delightful relaxation. Rumour has it that if you sail down the river, inland, for a while you will find a small island, where a recording studio was said to be. I may take a look one day. Hell, might even go for a job there.

I could while away my days listening to music – discovering new bands. Yeah, I can see it now – wait, no. That's stupid. I'm too old and tone deaf.

The wind and rain made the day darker than ever and allowed me to see my reflection in the window or the pub I was drowning my sorrows in.

Am I getting older? Of will I stay the same? I looked down at my fish and chips. Do I need to eat? Or sleep? I wake up every time in the Beast feeling the same, no sense of physical fatigue or drowsiness. The same levels of hunger and thirst that I had the time before, and the time before that.

I've been over these thoughts so many times now, it's just a part of me. Like the knowledge of your past, it's always there to remind you of where you came from.

God, this food looks like a heart attack on a plate. And the beers don't add much to the health kick either.

But to hell with it. It tastes great.

Is it wrong to just be selfish? Do you know what? I don't care anymore. I couldn't give a flying, well you know what.

I just want time for myself. I don't want the responsibility. I don't want the pressure, and I sure as hell don't want to keep dying anymore.

As a gazed out of the window, I watched the rain bounce off of the water where the boats were moored and realised. *That's what I want. I want to sail away. Sail away with nothing more than the shirt on my back, as if nothing else matters.*

Something hits the decking outside. I stood up and went over to the window. A seagull was lying dead on the floor, a pool of blood seeping out from underneath it.

I looked around and three more birds had suffered the same fate.

"It's the radiation." I turned to see an old man sitting at the bar.

"Excuse me?"

"That's what makes the birds drop. They say it's already moving across Europe. Millions could die in the first year they reckon." He took a sip of his beer. He looked like a man who had spent his whole life down here. His skin was leathered from the sun and he wore clothes that suggested he was at peace with himself. "Where you from, son?"

"I'm American, sir. US Secret Service."

He looked me up and down. "What you doing here then?"

I took a large gulp of my beer. "I'm getting out."

He studied me for a while. Everything about his screamed *I'm taking my time*.

"Don't blame you, son, don't blame you." He turned back the bar and took his beer glass. "Feel sorry for that family though. Must be terrible to lose them all like that."

I gave him a puzzled look.

"That Sallymac girl. You know, McDonald's wife? Lost her husband when he was shot in front of the palace, and her kids too. Tragic, if you ask me."

That snapped me out of my stupor. "What do you mean, kids?"

"Their kids, boy and girl. They were on holiday on the other side of London. Tried to get them to safety but didn't make it. Tragic if you ask me."

I downed the rest of my pint and went outside. The air was heavy with moisture.

I took a walk out along the boardwalks and out to the water breakers. I just wanted to stare out to sea.

I walked along the pier, past more bars and restaurants, and shops selling tourist gifts until I was moving along with just water either side of me.

I reached the mouth of the water breakers; the mouth of the dock where the civilization of the land meets the pure natural wildness of the sea.

The ocean was moving, pulsating, as though it were alive. And, I suppose it was.

I tried to work out of the tide was coming in or out, but I couldn't tell. The waves looked violent and unpredictable.

A small pleasure boat came put-put-putting past me, with a man at the helm, and a woman and two small children huddled together on the back seat.

As it moved slowly past me, we waved.

"Wouldn't stay too long there, mate," called the man. "Sea looks rough. You'll be swept away."

Just to prove his point, the ocean sent a spry up over me, covering me in a fine layer of salty water.

"Thanks. I'll get back to shore." I waved at the kids as they waved back at me.

"You can't stay here either. They say it's coming. From London. The radiation. We all need to evacuate."

He had stopped his boat just beneath me. "Where are you staying, friend? It's time to get out of here if you ask me."

I looked at the family at my feet, fleeing to get to safety, the honest concern in all their eyes at a stranger's safety.

I felt a lump in my throat.

"I couldn't save them."

"Excuse me."

"I said, I couldn't save them."

"What do you mean?" The woman was straining to hear me over the wind and the waves.

I hung my head in shame. "I gave up. I left them all to die back there."

The woman looked at me with a sense of pity. Her mothering nature shone through as she reached out with her voice to help me, even though I was a man in a suit standing on a pier; clearly not belonging, but still one of them.

She smiled and tilted her head to the side. "I'm sure you did all you could, but you need to come down from there. Please. You will be swept away. Here. Climb aboard and we'll take you back to safety."

She held out her hand as I began to step forward.

I paused at the edge of the boat. I looked at the children. They looked frightened.

"I still could save them all, if I wanted, you know."

"What?" The wind was really picking up, and she cupped her hands to her ears.

"Sorry, didn't catch that. Looks like a storm is coming." She beckoned me over.

"The storm. All of it, it's my fault."

She shook her head, the wind roared even louder.

"Whatever it is, it would be better if you just climb aboard. Just a quick jump, we'll all be safe."

"Exactly," I said as I stepped away from her, turned back to the sea, and swan dived into its welcoming arms.

Fourteen

I had gotten into an argument with Gina. Her instincts were to get out; just pack up and get the hell out of dodge. She was adamant that she wanted to evacuate, which I could understand, given what she was seeing unfold in front of her. And I didn't blame her, but I knew what was about to go wrong if we carried on down the same path. I was trying to convince her to buy me more time.

"…by retreating, by pulling back we will accelerate the timeframe."

"So, what do you suggest?"

"Let things play out without interruption."

"And let McDonald and Li get shot?"

"Yes, I know it sounds bad, but any intervention gets Gim mad, and we speed up the events. I need to work out how to stop them first, then go back and do it."

Gina rubbed her temples. She was pacing around the room, but sat down and undone the top button at the neck of her shirt. "OK, do we have any idea where these guys are? The only way to stop them is to find them."

I went over to the window. I could see the lawn with Marine One sat dead centre. I looked up at the sky which was now a dark grey. Something was definitely changing. *Did it matter that the weather was getting worse? What did that mean?* I contemplated these thoughts for a moment. But as I did my mind turned to something else. There was another problem that was staring us in the face. Something that had been bugging me for a while, but didn't want to face up to it. I turned to look at Gina. "What about me?"

Gina had her head in her hands and looked up when I spoke. "What about you?"

I went over and sat opposite her. "So far, every time I die, I end up back in the rear seat of the Beast, en route to the palace."

She leaned back in her chair and gazed at the ceiling. "And…?"

"And how do we know that this won't stop happening? Even in years to come?"

She sat bolt upright, eyes searching back and forth as she processed this new idea. "So, when you finally make it to that rocking chair with the grandkids on your knee…"

"And die of natural causes…"

"Shit."

I moved around the table and sat next to her. Our eyes meeting. "Everything resets and we are back here. No matter if it is twenty, thirty years from now. I'm forty-two again and having this exact same conversation."

She sighed as the realisation swept over her. "So, none of this matters. Whatever we do now, if we save the day, if we find Gim and stop all of this, it will all be undone. All of it."

Of all of the problems we were trying to overcome, this seemed like the biggest.

She was right. Unless I could fix this, none of it mattered. The world would still go to hell in a handcart.

As if on cue, a rumble came from outside. Both of us jumped up and looked out of the window. "The power plant again?"

Gina was scanning the skyline for any tell-tale signs.

"No. It's worse than that. It's thunder."

She raised an eyebrow. "You worried about the weather now? You need a break."

She was trying to lighten the mood, something I was grateful for. I was glad Gina was with me on this, I needed someone else to lighten the load; take some of the burden. But this was another problem, just about as big as the others.

"When all this started, it was hot and sunny. Beautiful day. Not a cloud in the sky. I was sweating in my suit; a hot summer's day. Now there's a storm coming. It's been slowly turning this way. I hadn't noticed at first, but the weather had been getting slowly worse and worse; now there's thunder."

Sure enough, rain was starting to hit the window we were looking through, and the sky was dark, the promise of more rain to come. "Same date and time, but something is shifting. I have no idea if it is linked to me resetting time, but it feels like the universe is trying to tell me something. Like it's angry, like I've broken something in time."

"So what do we do?"

Gina stood and put on her jacket. I looked up as she made for the door. "Where are you going?"

"Come on. We need more help."

Fifteen

Gina and I walked down through to the basement of Winfield House. She had access to the building as part of her role in the Service, and we had snagged the keys to the garage.

We had given the other guys in the operations room the slip – to be honest they won't notice our absence for a while, given the drama that was about to command their attention in a few minutes.

Gina was marching along the corridor, with me trying to keep up. "We will only have the official cars available to us. But once the grid goes down, we will have the charge in the batteries and that's it."

"What do we do once the charge runs out? If the grid goes down doesn't the navigation and bio security drop also?"

Gina winked at me as we entered the garage. "Guess we'll need an alternative then."

She walked over to the small security booth in the corner, opened the door and grabbed a set of keys. We went over to the corner where there was a small car with a tarp cover. It didn't look much bigger than a go kart. "Give me a hand?" she said as she undid the cables around the wing mirrors.

We pulled back the cover to reveal a small open top roadster. I stood and admired the sleek lines, the chrome spoked wheels and the overall aesthetic beauty before asking "What is it? An Aston Martin?" I ran my fingers over the bonnet and along the door sill.

"No. E Type jag. 1961 3.8 litre roadster." She was grinning at the vehicle in front of us as she continued. "Steel chassis, aluminium body, chrome details with an inline six-cylinder dual overhead camshaft, all leather seats and finished in British racing green. Enzo Ferrari called it the greatest car ever made."

A let out a low whistle. "Old car. Wait, does this run on fossil fuels?" Gina was allowing herself a moment to stare at is just as I was. "Does it still run?"

"One way to find out." Gina inserted the key into the lock on the door and turned it.

The top was down, and we opened the doors and sat in the red leather seats, my legs barely fitting in the footwell.

"And this is an 'official' car?" I did the bunny ears as I said it.

Gina shrugged her shoulders. "It was back in the day. Guess they never updated the records. Oh, and by now it will be worth around twenty to thirty million." She shot me a serious look. "Don't scratch it." I instinctively pulled by hands away from the leather door trim as Gina put the key in the ignition and started it first time. The roar of the old fuel burning engine reverberating around the walls like a caged tiger waiting to get out. I jumped at the sound. The smell of the oils filling my senses and the vibration of the car sending shivers all over my body. I felt a smile creep across my face.

"Reminds me of old movies. Can you drive this?"

Gina looked down at the stick coming out of the floor between us. "It's been a while." She adjusted the mirrors and touched a few of the switches on the dash. "My dad used to restore these back home, when I was a little girl. These old cars have a gearbox that you have to change in sequence with the clutch pedal. Let's see now…"

She worked the controls, and after a couple of crunching noises, we started moving forward. The noise as she pressed the throttle increased and we rumbled forward. It sounded glorious. It made me think what it must have been like when London was full of noises like these. It must have been loud and wonderful at the same time. We turned and headed for the exit ramp, as the gate swung open automatically to let us out.

"Wonder if they'll realise we've gone?" I shouted above the engine as we pulled out.

"Probably. But they can't track us in this." She gunned the car and the purr changed to a roar as we swung out of the rear of Winfield House and headed south out of London.

We headed away from Hyde Park, as to avoid the crowds around the palace, and cut through Mayfair, Carnaby Street and Covent Garden to get to Westminster Bridge.

Driving in this car, through the old cobbled streets that I am glad that they have kept in London, it felt incredible. We got more looks than the presidential motorcade driving in this drop top; not caring for the rain as we just wanted to see and be seen.

People filmed us, and took photos as we left the West End, and crossed the river by the Houses of Parliament.

The buildings and crowds were quickly left behind as we entered more rural areas, and soon, they disappeared too.

As we left the outskirts of the commuter belt, I was able to take in the beautiful English countryside. Buildings melted away and were replaced by rolling green fields. Sheep and cows barely flinched as we flew past them.

We were on a single lane road that snaked its way through the ebb and flow of the countryside. A ribbon of asphalt that laid lazily over the rolling fields and meadows, inviting the driver to throw the car into the bends, caressing the corners as the engine purred in appreciation.

The rain was subsiding, and the sun started to break through as we headed for the coast, shafts of light permeated the sky as a cool breeze blew though my hair, refreshing me as we drove south.

For the first time in what felt like half a lifetime, I allowed myself a moment to relax as I gazed at the scenery as we whooshed past, engine burbling and spitting, the car feeling as alive as I did.

We stuck to the single lane country roads to not get spotted, and also to avoid the panic traffic of people trying to escape the chaos of London.

The radio would only receive signals from a bygone era, so we had to rely on sight to assess the traffic situation, and once or twice our winding country road passed under a motorway flyover, and we saw and heard nothing but traffic and horns blaring.

We had no sat nav and had turned our phones off so we couldn't be found, so we were navigating using road signs and landmarks. Doing it the old-fashioned way.

Most road signs had overgrown or had faded away, as all modern drivers didn't need them, but here, in this wonderful machine, we felt like explorers using nothing but the world around us to navigate, like old ships captains used to use the stars.

"How far are we?" The first thing I had said in nearly half an hour.

Gina chuckled to herself. "The kids are getting restless on this road trip."

She pointed at a spot over on the hill. "See that old church?" I looked at where she was pointing, an old-fashioned steeple was disappearing from view as we dipped into a valley, the weather vane gently moving in the breeze.

"Hart lives in an old farmhouse a few miles further south. Had been held up in there ever since North Korea. Said he wanted to be permanently off grid."

I stuck my hand out to the side, to feel the push of the air as we raced along. "Heard he went crazy," I said, knowing the response.

"Yeah, and then some."

We carried on driving; the church was much bigger on our left-hand side. Now we were close, I could see it was a ruin. Old stone walls were crumbling, and the spire was just about the only thing left standing; and that was slowly losing its fight with gravity. It leaned with the cadence of a drunk trying to make his way home after a night out, listing steadily to one side as it stumbled down the road.

"Do you think it is possible?" I ask. Gina glanced sideways at me. "To go off grid, I mean. Can it really be done, in today's day and age?"

Gina leant one arm out to the side, catching the breeze in her palm and allowing it to surf the air like a wave. "Hart thinks he has. But you have to able to live off the land. As soon as you pay for something, or even go out into the next town, you are on a database, or on camera. As you say; today's day and age. Almost impossible."

We swung off the road and onto a dirt track. The car was kicking up a trial of dust as we entered a hollow in the trees. The dappled sunlight momentarily dazzled us before the space opened up into a clearing, where an old stone farmhouse was sat all alone. Gina parked the car about a hundred feet from the house and killed the engine.

She turned to me in the seat and pocketed her glasses. "Something you should know about Hart," she began. "He has been alone for a while. The last time I saw him he was… odd."

"Define odd," I said. Gina was about to reply, but one of the windows at the top of the house opened, and the barrel of a shotgun appeared.

"Who are you?" said Hart, a dishevelled head of hair could be seen behind the weapon.

"That kind of odd," said Gina as we calmly and slowly got out of the car, our hands above our heads.

"It's me, Gina. Del Fonte. I've got Doctor Hill with me."

Silence permeated the house for a moment, then the gun withdrew inside. Moments later, the front door opened, and, still holding the shotgun, David Hart appeared, walking slowly towards us, still pointing the firearm at our heads, switching between me and Gina as he approached.

He was wearing jeans, a plaid shirt and had wild brown hair. He sported a scruffy unkempt beard, and his hands were greasy; black dirt was under his fingernails and was also visible in streaks over his face. The face of a man who worked with machinery, and didn't have any human contact.

"Prove it," he said in a croaky voice. "Prove you are her."

"David," Gina said as she lowered her hands. "I was here a year ago. We had tea. You told me about your research."

I looked to her and back to Hart. He may be dishevelled, but his stare was unflinching. Military training.

Hart lowered the gun and let out a huge belly laugh. "I'm just messing with you, of course I know who you are. Come here!"

He gave her a huge embrace; the way old friends greet each other.

"You remember Dr Hill. He was in the field hospital."

I extended my hand. "Please, Gibson." We shook as he looked me in the eye.

"Yes, I remember you. You were lead doctor in the unit in North Korea. That yours?" he said, looking over to the Jaguar.

"No, we stole it from the US embassy."

He let out another belly laugh. "Nice! They deserve everything they get."

"David, we are here because we need your help." She paused before collecting her thoughts. "Dr Hill, Gibson here. Well, he…" She seemed to struggle to know where to begin.

"I'm experiencing the same things as you did in North Korea."

David Hart studied me for a moment. "Well," he said, throwing an arm over my shoulder. "You had better come inside. This requires tea."

Sixteen

We sat at the old wooden table and drank tea as I explained everything that had been happening. Hart interjected every so often with questions, interrogating the detail as I spoke. When I got to the moments when I returned back to the Beast, he became the most animated he had been since we arrived.

"What did it feel like, moments before you went back?"

I had to stop and think for a moment. "It didn't feel like anything. One minute I was wherever I was, and the next I was back in the rear seat with Salanski, Turner and Li. It was like I just woke up from a daydream."

He was leaning forward in his chair now, getting as close to my face as the table would allow.

"Yes, yes, but… when you died. How did that feel. Did you feel the pull? The gravity of it all? The sense of falling and flying at the same time. And when you woke up, did it feel like being reborn? Like your life had ended and you were given another chance?"

I smiled a nervous smile as I said, "No. Not really. It was all so fast, just like a scene cut in a movie. Didn't have time to feel anything."

He rocked back. "Hmm… so you didn't stay in limbo for a period then?"

"Excuse me?

He was playing with his beard as he spoke. "Well, when this happened to me, in Korea, between when I died, and came back, I was… nowhere."

"Nowhere?"

"Yes, yes… I called it limbo. I was kind of… well… floating."

"What do you mean – some kind of purgatory?"

"You could call it that I suppose. But I wasn't anywhere. I was just floating. There was nothing around me, but I could see myself. I tried to count out how long, I reckon it was about two hours at one point."

"Wow." I was silent for a while as I searched my memories. "No. For me it was instantaneous. You must have wondered if…"

"If I would ever come back? Yeah. Can you imagine the first time it happened? I was shit scared."

We sat and drank tea for a moment until David snapped us out of our funk. "Anyway, continue, please."

I carried on explaining my story. For the rest of it Hart largely let me talk as I got to the points about the attacks in London, and how I had tried in vain to prevent them from happening.

"So you see… we need your help. Gina tells me you figured out what is happening, and how to fix this."

Hart stood up and paced the kitchen. "I *knew* it. I *knew* I wasn't crazy. I told them. I told them all, but they wouldn't believe me. Said I was hallucinating. Said I couldn't possibly see the future. But I tell you, I was there. Every time I was killed in battle, I was back to the start of the day. Over and over again. Not one person would listen. Not one!" He put his hands in the counter, looked out the window to the farm outside.

"How did you get out?" I asked.

He watched the chickens walk around the farm outside. They all pecked at the ground as they looked for food, picking at the dirt as they moved. I followed his gaze to the animals. They reminded me of the people in the city we had just left behind. Everyone scurrying around looking out for themselves. Everyone in the same race for food and shelter. Oblivious to what could be about to happen.

"I was honourably discharged from the army," he began. Voice steady and calm. "After we pushed back the insurgents in North Korea, I tried to tell them how we did it. How I had the 'foreknowledge' to know the future. Thought I was suffering from PTSD."

"So you were kicked out?"

"Yeah."

"But how did that stop the… your situation?"

He came over and sat at the table opposite me. "Give me your hand."

I looked at Gina, who shrugged her shoulders. I put my hand on the table.

Hart pulled out a knife, and before I could pull back, grabbed my wrist and slashed the palm of my hand. Gina stood, her chair flying backwards as she rose, gun already aimed at Hart's head.

"Relax, Del Fonte." He waved her away with his hand as she cocked the hammer back and moved around behind him.

"Just watch."

I looked at my hand as the wound was already knitting closed. The familiar tingling sensation passing across my palm.

Hart took my hand once more and ran his thumb over the skin where you could hardly see a mark. "Hmm. Best I've seen." He pulled my hand closer as he pulled a pair of glasses from his top pocket and studied the flesh more closely.

"Yes, best I've ever seen."

Gina had sat back down again. Her gun holstered. "You're carrying nano."

Hart released his grip on my wrist.

"Thought they only gave that out to a select few people. You must have slept with the right person."

He had a twinkle in his eye that took ten years off him.

"I'm on a trial. Clinical one. They needed test patients." I could feel the burning eyes of Gina. "I needed the money. So what?"

"Let me guess," said Hart. "Craven?"

Doctor Craven was a notorious figure in the nano tech field. His developments in medicine had revolutionised warfare, but his methods were dangerous. Often conducting illegal experiments on subjects that would result in horrific disfiguration, and, in some cases, catastrophic organ failure. Patients dying in excruciating agony.

But, needless to say, he was struck off and put on trial for his crimes. Craven never made the trial though. He hung himself in his cell before he made it to the docks.

"Yes."

Gina looked horrified. "He was a madman. You let *him* give you a trial tech drug?"

I felt my blood boil as I was forced to defend myself. "It was before we knew what he was up to! Before any of the revelations had come out!"

"Jeez, Gibson. No wonder you are having a weird episode."

"Oh, you try it for a while and see what happens!" I had stood up and was squaring up to Gina. Even though I was taller and heavier than her, she stood her ground; used to a world of men trying to intimidate her.

Hart broke up our brewing fight. "Guys, guys. This gets us nowhere. Dr Hill; Gibson." He said, "When did you go on this trial?"

"Just after North Korea."

"Makes sense. Just you?"

"I think so. In my trial at least."

Gina was listening to our back and forth, rubbing her temples as we spoke. "So you are saying it's the nano tech? That sounds impossible. How does the nano do all of this?" she said, pointing at me.

"All I know is a new AI was being developed by Craven," said Hart. "Said he had created a new defence mechanism that responds to threat."

"New defence?"

"Said it could evolve."

"Ridiculous." Gina spoke into her cup as she drank her tea; trying to process what we were saying.

"OK, but how do I get this out? How did *you* get *yours* out?"

Hart grabbed his coat and walked to the door. "Well come on then."

"Come on what?"

"I have something in my barn to show you."

Seventeen

We walked across the farm and over to an old dilapidated-looking barn. But when we entered, I was shocked at what was hidden in there.

The floor was just the bare dirt covered in thin strands of old hay. The wooden slats that made up the walls were broken in places, and creaked in the breeze, hinting at structural failure with alarming regularity.

Indeed, every time the wind blew, there was a metal-on-metal scrape from somewhere unseen, high up above, and a thin trickle of sawdust floated down from the ceiling, adding to the neat pile on the floor just in front of my feet.

I checked for the exits.

My eyes were drawn to the centre of the room, where a large steel column ran from floor to ceiling. It was a structure comprised of high-grade pylons arranged in a circle, about three feet in diameter, with cables running up and down inside.

Placed in front was a wooden table and on it was a laptop, with a larger screen bolted onto the pylons at head level.

Hart went around behind the central structure and climbed a wooden ladder up to an upper platform that had what looked like an old truck engine. Hart turned a few valves, checked a few dip sticks and pressed a button.

The engine fired into life. Deeper and louder than the Jaguar we drove here in, and shook the already creaky barn even more than the wind outside.

The centre console sprang to life, lights climbed up and down the cabling like ants running along a tree.

As Hart skidded down and reached the bottom of the ladder, he started pushing a dentist-like chair over towards us. He came around to our side with a set of notes in his hands. "All self-contained power," he offered as an

explanation. "Doesn't need the grid so I can't be detected."
He made a groaning sound much like the barn as he pulled
one of the cables from the central pylon and connected it to
the bottom of the chair.

"Could have made it louder," offered Gina.

Hart ignored the sarcasm, and carried on connecting up
the chair, before moving over to the laptop. The screen came
on and a graphic of the chair appeared on the left, with a
series of graphs on the right. All of them worryingly showed
a flatline.

"OK, Gibson, take a seat." He beamed at me and
gestured for me to sit.

I looked at Gina and didn't move. "What is it?"

Hart ruffled his hair, his voice getting faster and higher
with every word he spoke. "Yes, yes, sorry. I took some
ideas from the hospital whilst in Korea. Medical bay. Well,
a crude attempt at any rate." He glanced up and scratched
his beard. "Oh, perfectly safe, just diagnostics. For now.
Please, sit. I just want to interrogate the nano."

Gina was shifting her weight from side to side. "You've
used this on yourself?" I could see where she was going.

"Oh yes, don't go into hospitals you see. I would be on
record. They'd know where I am. Or that I'm still alive."
He looked up at Gina who was slightly shaking her head.
"Oh, you mean – have I done anything to myself with it?
Yes, of course. Keep my cholesterol in check with it. Also
fixed a small fracture in my arm once. Fell from the upper
deck," he said, gesturing up to where the engine was still
throbbing away.

"Gina," I said, walking over to the chair. "I'm sure it's
OK. Just need to see what's going on. Right, David?"

"Exactly, yes. Please. Oh, and could you remove your
top half please?"

"Top half?"

"Yes, jacket, shirt. I need to place the contacts on skin."

I stripped to the waist and handed my clothes to Gina,
who slung them over an old wheelbarrow next to her.

He held the headrest of the chair as I lay back and he strapped my arms down to the rests.

"Is this really…"

"Necessary? I need you to stay perfectly still when we scan."

I saw Gina instinctively touch her hip where her gun was holstered.

Hart pulled a cable out of the pylon, the loose end finishing in a small strap, which he secured around my upper arm.

He moved over to the console and started punching keys on the keyboard.

"Right then, let's take a look, yes?" I noticed that a figure of a person was now laying in the chair graphic, and a stream of data was scrolling along the display and graphs.

"Oh yes, very, very interesting. Oh my. Oh yes."

He twisted the screen round to face me, and Gina moved to my side to take a view.

"OK, you see this?" said Hart, pointing to a series of numbers on one of the graphs. I shrugged as well as I could in my straps.

"It's just as I suspected. You have the new nano tech. Even newer that the one I was given actually." I detected a note of envy in his voice. "And it is capable of a level of sentient thought I have not seen before."

"You mean, it can think?" Gina looked as though the blood had drained from her face.

"There's more. It has connected to you at a quantum level. More than mine ever did; much more in control."

"Meaning?"

"Meaning you weren't kidding about weird shit happening!"

"But can you turn it off?"

David was bouncing on his toes. Animatedly typing as he spoke. "It is possible I can reprogram, but I have never tried with that level of sophisticated nano before."

"Is there a risk to Doctor Hill?" Gina was pacing around the old barn in front of me.

"Gina, it's OK. Let David have a try at least." I addressed Hart, who was pacing back and forth. "Try anything you think might work."

He stopped pacing as he came to a conclusion. "OK. We have to reprogram."

"Reprogram?"

"Yes, well, you see. It is doing a lot of things for you. You know, fixing minor injuries, monitoring your vitals."

"Like most nano does in the field, right?"

"Yes, but this is a heavily modified. To protect you. It has evolved to do such a great job of getting you out of an impossible situation, it is actually throwing you back along your own timeline. Amazing, really."

"So this could go on forever?" asked Gina.

"Yes, but…" Hart stopped typing and looked at me gravely.

"What is it, David?" asked Gina.

"The shock to your body every time you are pulled back is extreme. You are ripping a hole into the past and jumping through. The nano is also helping protect you. Without it you would be ripped to pieces by the sheer force."

"Nice. Where do I sign up for the next one?"

"This is no laughing matter. You need to keep this in your system or the forces you have been experiencing would quickly overwhelm you. It is still holding everything at bay. Even now."

Gina asked the next question. "Does that mean yours was doing them same thing?"

"I had minor effects in Korea. After about ten jumps I had figured out how to win the battle. Got it out in time… wait." He leant over me so our noses were almost touching. "How many times did you say you had jumped?"

I was struggling to remember. "About fifty, sixty. Maybe more. I lost count."

Hart stood and looked solemnly down at me. "Then I am afraid you don't have long left."

"Gibson, I'm so sorry," said Gina. Her eyes were glistening as she said it.

"There is only one option then." Both looked at me. "David, can this be reprogrammed to go back further? Send me back and extra hour?"

"The forces would be devastating. You wouldn't survive."

"But it can be done?" He rubbed his beard as he composed his thoughts. "In theory, but I doubt you would—"

"Survive? Is there something that can help?"

He pushed his hands into his pockets as he thought. "No. No, there is no survival."

"How long would it take? How long would I have to do what I need to?"

"It really is unknown. But at a best guess; I can see you are already in trouble. The nano is repairing constantly, but any further back and it raises exponentially. An extra hour is possible, but anymore and you would rapidly decline. How quickly, I could not say for certain. But you would have days. Weeks at most."

"OK, do it."

"Gibson, please think about this." Gina had grabbed my hand.

"What choice is there? You said yourself, this will happen forever otherwise."

She crouched down in front of me. "But what if something happens? What if he…"

She pulled back as her shoulders slumped. The realisation on her face was something I had seen already. "We've been here before, haven't we?"

Hart stopped doing what he was doing on the terminal and looked over at me. He shelved his notes and looked at me through his steel-rimmed glasses. "How many times?"

I let out a sigh. The smell of the fumes from the engine was getting to me. How did those people back in the old days drive cars with these things on board? "This is the fourth time we have had this conversation."

I lay my head back on the chair and gathered my thoughts. My memory now a blur of the same events repeated over and over again.

"The first two times you tried to extract the nano, but both times it instantly reacted, and I was back in the Beast."

"And what about the last time?" asked Gina.

"Tried to reprogram to send me back an hour earlier."

"Like I am about to now?"

"Yes, but you said there would be two ways of doing it."

"Yes." David pointed at the screen with my body outline on it. "One way is to reprogram the code. Reset the clock, so to speak."

"Doesn't work. Nano seems to know that one."

"OK, then the other is to try and give it a new command. A new command to tell it where the safe point is."

"Safe point?" asked Gina.

"Yes, you see every time it detects Doctor Hill is in mortal danger, it sends him back to the last known point that it knew you were completely safe."

"Like in the back of an armoured convoy."

"Exactly."

"So we tell it that the Beast isn't safe."

Hart started typing furiously as he spoke. "We can potentially do it. Need to find a new safe point. Winfield House an hour earlier seems logical. I think I have the correct time coordinates."

"Gibson, are you sure about this?" Gina was doing her best, but I knew the consequences better than anyone.

I allowed myself to close my eyes, my mind had been a racing hive of activity for how long, I had lost track. All I wanted to do was sleep. Maybe even dream of something warm and relaxing. I knew that this nightmare would now only end in one way, and I had resigned myself to the facts.

"David," I said, "please send me back an extra hour." I looked at Gina. "I'll find you as soon as I can. I should arrive in Winfield House."

"Done," said David. "Just wait for it to load in."

"Done?" Gina looked surprised. "That was fast."

"Just changed the coding. It is a computer program after all." He gave us a childlike grin as he came over to join Gina next to my bed.

"Thanks buddy," I said. "I owe you a crate of beer or two." The computer bleeped behind Hart, so he motioned for Gina to stand back, and both her and Hart waited in anticipation.

After a moment, David spoke. "Aren't you supposed to dematerialise, or something?"

"Come on now, David, you know what has to happen." I looked at Gina, who realised her fate.

"Please, Gina. Do me one last favour. Shoot me in the head."

Eighteen

I came to and instantly knew something was wrong. The pain in my head was more intense than the worst hangover I had ever had.

The light hurt my eyes, my heart was having palpitations and I could feel my shirt getting wet with sweat.

The rocking motion of the car wasn't helping either; I have never had the strongest stomach, so the combination of all these things was making me nauseous.

I decided to sit there a moment and hide behind my shades and slow my breathing.

The road noise was comforting, and the radio was playing a nice tune.

As I came to my senses a little, I realised what was really bugging me. A nagging in the back of my head, like a little itch that was needing to be scratched was calling out and slowly demanding my attention as we rolled along.

Come on, it said. *You know what it is. It's obvious. Plain as the nose on your stupid, dim-witted face.*

Sat in the car a little longer, trying to process my thoughts.

Car. I'm in the Beast? The itch grew louder. *You were sent back a whole hour earlier.* I sat forward and rubbed my temples. *Should you be in the Beast yet?* Still with my eyes closed, I rubbed the back of my neck.

That's it, sailor, said the voice in my head. *Hear that? That's the sound of a penny dropping.*

"You OK, babe?" The voice opened my eyelids like a roller blind shooting up the window.

Stephanie leant forward from the opposite seat of the cab and put her hand on my leg and gave it a rub. "You look awful. Are you OK?"

I took off my glasses and looked around us. *We were in a London Black Cab. I remember this. This is the week before. I have overshot by a long way. David got this way wrong.*

"Babe? Talk to me?" She was looking worried.

She was my girlfriend. Well, a girl that I used to date in London, but we had that kind of off, on, off kind of thing going on. This was a clear five days before I needed to be here. We had met up in London to try one more time, but it had ended in a big fight one evening at dinner in a restaurant near the river, after we had taken a taxi tour of the city. *This* evening, in fact.

This is good, right? I have time. But at what cost? Will I make it through the next few days?

"Yes, I'm…" With the first time I tried to speak, it all started swirling around in my head. Before I could stop, I threw up all over the taxicab floor.

"Ah for Christ's sake, mate!" The cab driver was twisting in his seat. "Who's gonna clean that up?"

I tried to speak, but the world span again. I must have blacked out, or partially at any rate, as all I could hear was Stephanie arguing with the cab driver. "…then please just take us to St Thomas'… I'll pay for the cleaning bill, just get there, please…"

A blacked out fully.

Nineteen

I came to in a hospital bed. There was a drip in my arm, and a view of London out of the window. I could see out to the river, where tourist boats and barges meandered their way along, creating a gentle wake in their path.

On the other side of the river was the Houses of Parliament. Rebuilt after a fire in the 1840s, it has stood as a monument to British politics for centuries. Even surviving the infamously foiled plot by Guy Fawkes to blow it up, and ironically still celebrated by the Brits as Fireworks Night, on November the 5th.

The grand clock tower on the right of the Palace of Westminster, as it is formally known, played out its famous peel of bells, and the most famous of those bells, Big Ben, chimed three times.

I tried to sit, but the nausea prevented me. A nurse on her rounds spotted me and came over to my cubicle. "Good afternoon," she said in a cheery tone. It always amazed me how medical professionals managed to keep an upbeat tone in the face of what must be a lot of pain and suffering.

"Looks like someone is awake. How are you feeling?"

I managed to sit this time, with the aid of a pillow the nurse stuffed behind me to help prop me up. "Like I could throw up." Even as I spoke, I could feel the bile rising. "Please, what day is it? How long have I been here?"

The nurse was checking my vitals on the machine next to me. "Wednesday, my love. You have been in here overnight. I would say it is a nice day outside, but since you came in, we have been having nothing but rain." As she said this last part, she pulled a silly face, but my sense of humour had left me.

"I have that effect on the weather."

"Well, we'll try and brighten you up at least, my love." She was trying her best, I suppose.

At that moment the doctor walked in, absorbed in his hand-held tablet. He looked up when he saw me and stopped reading, and came to sit on the chair next to me. "Good morning, I'm Doctor Knight. And I believe you are Doctor Gibson Hill?"

I nodded my agreement. Too much talking was bad for my constitution.

"Your partner…" he scrolled through his notes, "…Steph brought you in last night with multiple complications that we are still trying to understand." He paused as I nodded once more. "I would like to understand what happened to you a little further, Doctor Hill, as I have to say – myself and my colleagues are baffled."

I had taken a sip of tea that the nurse had fetched for me, and was coming to my senses a little.

"There is no easy way to say this," he continued, "you are showing signs of organ failure and DNA damage right across your body. If I had been shown these results in any other situation, I would say you have acute radiation sickness, but we can find no evidence of radioactivity in your bloodstream, or skin or tissue damage that would be consistent with this." He took off his glasses and cleaned them on his shirt.

"Did you know this was happening to you prior to being admitted to this hospital? As I say, we were sent you medical records from the US, and I cannot see any mention of past issues like this in there."

My head was clearing, so I was able to sit more. "No, I didn't know about this."

I was not in the right frame of mind to conjure up any sort of convincing lie; I just wanted out of here.

"Well, what have you been up to the last few days? Anything out of the ordinary been going on? Taken any drugs, or been anywhere where you may have been exposed to anything hazardous?"

I coughed and put my cup to my lips. All I could do was shake my head.

"We did also discover that you are carrying military nano tech in your system; did you serve at all?" he asked.

"Korea," was all I could manage.

"Ah, military man then, good, good. Well unfortunately it looked to be very faulty, and causing some issues, and we couldn't reset it for some reason, so we have prepped a theatre to take you in and get it out."

That made me wake up. "You what?"

"Oh, don't worry, I've contacted your surgeon in the US, they can replace when you get home, but won't be until then. Just try and stay out of trouble for a few days, eh?"

The nurse had left for us to have some privacy, but had returned with a tray of food.

"Well, mustn't keep a man from his lunch. As I say, we must keep you in for a while until we can work up a treatment for you, so rest up and I'll talk to you later this evening."

As the doctor exited and the nurse arranged my food on the table, I looked down at the tubes and wires coming out of my arms, and could only think of one place I needed to get to.

Part 2 – Denial is the Key

Twenty

It was Thursday Morning. I had made it, somehow, to Winfield House and found Gina.

It was a much quieter affair the day before the NATO summit, and only some of the agents had arrived.

It didn't take me long to convince Gina this time, and we made plans to escape the grounds, but not before she got me to the medibay and gave me a series of vitamin shots to pep me up.

We snuck out under the pretence of taking me back to the hospital, and found the nearest cab to Battersea.

We had spent the night in a hotel just across the river from the power station, in Churchill Gardens, on Grosvenor Road.

We had insisted on a river front view room, and two single beds. We had raided Winfield House yesterday for gear we might need, including surveillance equipment, and guns. We had ditched our mobile phones and radios and scored enough food from the kitchens to keep us going so we didn't need cards in a cashless society.

We were now officially off grid.

I sat on the bed near the window as Gina assembled the equipment. She had set up two telescopic lenses; one pointing at the entrance of Battersea Power Station, and one pointed at the roads, and Chelsea Bridge, leading up to it.

We were on a stakeout.

The rain was pouring down, and every so often a crack of thunder shook the hotel we were in. Gina had set up the gear and was pulling one of the chairs over from the nearby desk; getting comfy for what could be a very long day.

She looked over at me and nodded at the seat next to her, but I was having problems of my own. I had a headache that had grown from bad yesterday evening, to migraine levels this morning.

My back was drenched in sweat and my palms were clammy. As I rose to move to the window, the room span, and I fell back onto the bed. I yelped and grabbed onto the sheets as it felt as though someone had flipped me upside down, even though my eyes told me I wasn't moving.

Gina came over to me. "What happened? What is it?"

I tried to sit, slowly so to control the nausea. "Vertigo," I said. "It'll pass."

Right on cue, it sent me into another spin, so I jumped up and made it to the bathroom and emptied my stomach into the toilet. *Stake outs aren't as glamourous as you see in the movies*, I laughed to myself.

I got to the seat by the window; and looking out to the river helped settle my mind down from the spinning.

The River Thames was snaking its way through London, and was a traffic thoroughfare serving the capital morning, noon and night. I watched a tourist boat as it unloaded its passengers at the power station pier, all of them drenched and tired looking with their ponchos and cameras.

A group of rowers skulled passed my view, and a large cargo vessel moved in the opposite direction, headed east to the centre of the city.

I slowly swung my telescope left, to move away from the bridge to the power station. The brown building and its four iconic towers were declared a listed building, and dated back to the Victorian times.

It had been refurbished and rebuild several times over the years, but always remained the same. The building work, fastidious in keeping the original, looks intact.

People of all nationalities were coming and going; tourists and workers were swarming amongst the crowds; the traffic on the roads outside was thick, and flowing.

I scanned further east and focussed in on the Stars and Stripes fluttering in front of the US Embassy.

In contrast to the power station, the Embassy building was modern in its design. A glass cube, surrounded by uniform translucent petal shaped crystalline structures; the building is surrounded by green spaces and water; a modern take on a working office.

As I watched the front of the embassy for a moment, I followed a group of foreign students as they took photos of everything around them. A security guard barked something at them – presumably to not take photos so close to the embassy.

My heart skipped a beat when I saw him. He had hand tattoos that I recognised straight away.

"Gina. Check the guard out front of the embassy." She swung her telescope over to where I was looking.

"What about him?"

"Last time I was close to him, he had his hands around my neck." She zoomed in a little closer. "He will jump the barriers and try and grab McDonald tomorrow. Get thrown in Paddington jail where I get to be his roommate if I so desire."

"OK, so he is a hostile. Doesn't mean he has anything to do with the Flowering Knights."

I looked up from my own telescope. "He wore a pig mask."

Gina stood and put her jacket on.

"Where are you going?"

"To take some pictures. Come on. Get changed. You look far too much like an agent." She took some items out of her bag and arranged them on the floor of our room.

"What are you doing?"

"Laying a trap. Get changed and let's go."

We walked over Chelsea Bridge looking as much like a pair of innocent tourists as we could. We had grabbed some clothes from a nearby shop, and I was in jeans, a pair of converses, an *I heart London* t-shirt and a very touristy rain proof poncho, completed with a rucksack I wore in front of me. I must have screamed *rob me* to any passers-by.

Gina somehow pulled off a different look. She had jeans like me, but had a simple shirt and leather jacket. She looked like the teacher to my student.

We walked along the river toward the embassy, and casually milled around the entrance until we found who we were looking for.

"Two o'clock," said Gina out of the corner of her mouth without looking at him.

I reached into my bag and produced a burner phone I had picked up earlier. I started taking pictures of anything and everything around me. I began with the views of the greenery behind, and them aimed it at the building.

Our tattooed friend took the bait immediately. He came striding over to us, blocking my view of the embassy with the palm of his hand. "You can't take pictures here, sir. You need to show me what you have photographed and delete."

Wow. The though police are out in force today.

Gina was quick to react. She spoke in a slow Southern drawl, and flashed a winning smile as she spoke. "Oh, I'm sorry, Officer. We didn't know you couldn't. We are just so in awe of the beautiful building, me and Billy Bob here wanted to capture the moment, that's all."

Billy Bob? She flashed her smile once again and turned to me. "Hey, honey, let's do as this gentleman says and show him your phone, shall we?" She tipped the guard a wink. "Just not the dirty ones of me, babe."

Just as planned, I brought up the pictures on the phone and handed it over to him. He skimmed through a few as we stood there in the rain. He stopped and pinched to zoom in on one. "What's this?" He flipped the phone over and held it to my face.

It was a photo of Gina in our hotel room standing by the door, just before we left earlier today, but we had put one of the pig masks we found in a tourist shop on the floor, on top of a pile of clothes.

"Just our hotel room, man." My southern drawl was a lot worse than Gina's. She cleared her throat to get me to stop talking.

"Oh, that's just little old me, darlin' just this morning in my new get up. Do you like it mister?" *She was good.* "I bet all the boys love these shots."

Her whole body language had changed, she was twirling her hair with one finger, and somehow had thrust her hip to the side and was twisting the ball of her foot on the ground, giving her the effect of a teenager. It honestly took years off her.

"You know what I mean. What's with the mask?" He was becoming aggressive.

I looked him in the eye and took a chance. "Hey, man," I said. Dropping the fake accent. "Just showing trust amongst friends, as they say. *Gyo u I sin.*"

I had taken a risk in using one of these phases, but I knew if he was truly in deep, this would get us in.

The Flowering Knights, or Hwarang, have five phrases they use, or *Precepts for Secular Life*. Gim had already used one of them previously, *Im jeon mu toe*, to mean *never retreat in battle*.

The phrase I had just used was the third, less aggressive precept which roughly translates as *exhibit trust and sincerity amongst friends*. It looked as though he had taken the bait. I could see him weighing us up and deciding what to do next.

He looked subtly over his shoulder, and then said "What of tomorrow?"

I replied with what I knew may work. "The war cry will be heard." Gina was silent next to me. "And then we will begin."

The guard, still holding my phone, clicked around for a moment, and then handed it back to me. "Use this," he said, and then just as quickly turned with his head down and headed back to the embassy.

Gina and I looked at the screen to see an app open called *EnkripChat*. Gina took the phone and started swiping through. "It's some sort of encoded networking app."

As she read through her eyes widened. "You weren't making this up. Coded signals. Talk of the speeches tomorrow at Buckingham Place." She stopped as the colour drained from her face.

"What? What is it?"

"Movements of McDonald tomorrow. The whole convoy route is there."

"Who posted it?"

She swiped for a second. "Someone called the 'Lynx'."

"I've heard that name before."

"Where?"

"In another version of today, Gim was tracked the day after tomorrow to an old house in France. Troops were sent in and he detonated a suicide bomb. His last words before he died was 'Remember the Lynx'."

"And that guard asked what of the Lynx just then. Who is it?"

"No idea. We could look it up, but logging in using my laptop would compromise our location."

"So, what do you suggest?"

"We ask in there," I said, pointing to the Embassy. "Just need to get changed first."

Twenty-one

We walked back up to the embassy building half an hour later in full Secret Service mode. We wore our earpieces (although they were not connected) and had our badges, and, most importantly, our shades.

As we entered the building I looked around in awe. The entrance we were in was known as the gallery, and displayed works of art along one expansive wall; with the polished marble floor and stone walls illuminated by the glass exterior on the opposite side. The seal of the embassy was engraved in the wall behind the security desk, and a long sweeping staircase faced us at the far end. The only blip on the landscape was a tower of scaffolding the was erected on the inside, for window cleaners to work their way along.

It's amazing how the right attitude, and the right swagger will get you in places and past security guards. You don't need to have an appointment, or the right credentials; you just need to go with confidence. We flashed our badges and waltzed straight past security with a 'Sorry sir, official Secret Service business' and demanded that we saw the head of the Defence Attaché.

After a short wait, a man dressed in a military uniform who introduced himself as Rear Admiral Daniel Donaldson appeared in the foyer, and after a short set of introductions, we were escorted up to his office.

Gina and I sat opposite him on one side of his desk, with him in a large leather chair, his hands clasped in front of him.

"So, what do I owe the honour of a visit from our friends in the Secret Service?"

"Well, sir," I began, "first of all, thank you for seeing us uninvited like this, sir. We appreciate your time and hope we don't…" Gina cleared her throat. "Yes, of course. We have intelligence that puts the president at risk at the NATO summit tomorrow. We have reason to believe that a radicalised group operating under the flag of the Hwarang in Korea are operating a sleeper cell here in London, and an individual, or individuals that call themselves the 'Lynx' has access to confidential records of the Secret Service, including the movements of the president; which leads us to believe we have a mole. We would like to gain access to your intelligence to understand who the Lynx is, and intercept them ahead of tomorrow's summit lunch at Buckingham Palace."

Donaldson sat back in his chair and stared at us for a moment. His now bulging waistline squashed up against his desk. The chair creaked as he moved, straining and groaning in duress at its occupant.

"You OK, son?" he asked as I sat and waited.

"Sir?"

"You don't look well. Kinda pasty, if you don't mind me saying."

I didn't want to have to make up any lies or excuses. Or, worse, get into a discussion about my ailing health, so, I opted for "It's been a long week."

"Hell yeah to that, my friend." He leant forward and pushed a button on the intercom on his desk. "Can someone get the chief security analyst in here. Security clearance alpha five."

"Yes, sir," came the reply.

We sat in awkward silence for a moment. The intercom broke into life once more. "Sir, the CA is in my office, shall I send them in?"

"No need, we'll come out." He stood and made his way to the door.

Gina leaned over to me. "What now?"

I shrugged my shoulders. "Don't know, seemed very easy though."

We walked out to find a young woman standing, flanked by two of the security guards, one I recognised straight away; the grin on his face suggested he knew he was in line for promotion for ratting out two Secret Service agents.

As soon as they saw us both guards pulled their guns. The woman in middle spoke. "I am head of the counter terrorism division at the embassy. You are under arrest for conspiracy to commit treason. Please come with us."

My vision was blurring over again, I could feel the nausea coming on. *Now is not the time.* I tried to send a signal to my brain to give me a break, but it wasn't listening.

Gina looked as if she was going to make a run for it, but we were blocked in. The only exit was behind the trio in front of us.

We looked at each other and put our hands over our heads. The action of the movement sent my head into a spin. I stumbled backwards, and fell over the desk of the secretary next to me.

A cold sweat broke out over my skin, and I could feel the rising tide coming up to my throat. I rolled onto my hands and knees, and vomited up all over the floor.

"Great. Who's gonna clean that up?" said the rear admiral. He addressed the woman in front of him. "We are compromised. If these two know what is going to happen, others may too."

"Do we abort, sir?"

"No. Bring the timeline forward. And deal with these two." He stepped over me and exited the room. I felt the rough hands of the guards lift me off my feet and drag me back into the office we had just came from. I was dumped back on the same chair I sat on earlier.

I was still trying to gain control of my body, and my head that was once again spinning.

A trembling, tingling adrenaline rush was spreading across my hands, the kind you get when you are really nervous, or about to throw up. As I had done the former, I came to a swift conclusion.

Before I could come to my senses, Gina was shouting. "Both of you, move over to the corner of the room, face the corner and lie on the floor, face down."

I turned to look, pain now exploding across my forehead, to see Gina walking behind the woman, holding her firmly by the arm and pointing a gun in her back. I looked and the woman's own gun was missing from her holster.

"Get up," Gina said, as she nodded to me. "Move to the door." She kept the gun trained on the woman at all times. "Give me the office key," she said to the woman she was now holding hostage, whose trembling hand held it up for her.

I mustered all of my strength and did as I was told. We backed toward the door, and Gina shoved the woman in the office and shut the door. She locked it and snapped the key off in the lock.

We were in the anterior office for the secretary, who mercifully had left her work station, but could be anywhere, possibly raising the alarm.

Gina tucked the gun under her jacket, and we moved out into the corridor.

We peered around the corner first, and checked for movement. Several people were walking back and forth, mostly looking at phones or tablets.

We waited for most of the people to leave our line of sight and walked as casually as we could, nodding courteously at office workers as they passed us by, barely giving us a second look.

We made it down the corridor to the lift and pushed the call button. The display above the door signalled it was on the fifth floor; we were on the second. It didn't move for while, then ticked over to four and stopped. I checked left and right. More people were walking towards us. Third floor. It had stopped again. To my right, a security guard came around the corner. When he saw us, he slowed and spoke into his lapel radio. The lift was taunting us, I was sure; but the doors finally opened with five occupants; two guys in suits got out, leaving three inside.

We nodded at them and stepped in. The lift was headed for the ground floor, and I watched as the number ticked down at an agonisingly slow pace.

I was aware of the guys next to us giving me a worried look. But I guess I would too, if I looked like I did – pale, sweating, and probably with some vomit down my tie.

We were at the front, and I stole a glance at the ID badge of the man to my left. Some kind of clerk.

A ping signalled that we had arrived at the bottom, and the doors slid open. People were milling around the foyer, but no one challenged us. We headed straight for the door, but as we did, the security guards stepped over to block our path.

I tried the same tactic as we did in the entrance earlier, by using authority and the claim of "Secret service business", but as soon as we were spotted, I also saw the rear admiral and his secretary pointing us out to the security guards.

Trapped. Like rats in a maze.

I looked around us and spotted an out. "Gina. Gun." Without looking she slipped out the revolver and passed it to me behind my back.

"On my mark, fake left." I pulled the gun and fired at the base of the window cleaner's scaffolding, at the same time I grabbed Gina and we leapt to our right hand side.

The scaffolding began to topple, and fall toward the centre of the atrium, sending the guards and the rear admiral scattering for cover. As the structure fell, we headed for the gap being produced between the falling window cleaners and the window.

We sprinted along the wall, shots now firing and making dents in the security glass as we hurtled along our maze.

As we hit the main desk, I fired another shot into the ceiling, causing the people in front of us to scatter, and bolted for the door.

We made it through the front entrance, and out onto the street, heading down to the river at a full sprint.

I could hear footsteps pounding behind us, but desk jobs don't compare to being in the field, my friend.

The streets were packed with tourists, and we managed to find cover in the crowds. A couple of quick lefts and rights, and we were close to the edge of the power station, using a delivery lorry as temporary cover.

"What did he mean by moving the timeline up?" Gina was breathing hard as she spoke.

"I think we better get inside here." I motioned up to the iconic towers of Battersea behind us.

"You think that it could happen today?"

"I don't know, but we need to warn them."

We agreed our next move and headed around to the river side of the building. Gina pulled out a small pair of binoculars that she had brought with her, and scanned the walls.

Just then I caught something moving on the embankment. I motioned to Gina and she zoomed in on the object.

A small red power boat was bobbing up and down by the pier. We edged closer to get a better view. Two men were on the boat, and another was passing a large black bag to them from the shore.

One of the men was clearly in charge, as he stood and watched the other two doing the loading work whilst he took a call on his phone.

Moving the timeline up?

"What is that?" I said as I squinted at the boat.

"Here," said Gina as she passed me the binoculars.

I could see black bags, and some silver cases. Some king of electrical equipment? Who knows? I refocussed on the men. I was able to get a better look at the faces on the boat. The two men I didn't recognise, but the one passing the bag was instantly familiar.

I handed the binoculars back to Gina. "It's them," I said.

"You're certain? You recognise those guys?"

My chest was still heaving, and I wanted nothing more than a warm bed and maybe a beer or two. The rain was pounding down heavily on me, and I was glad of its cooling effects.

"The two on the boat, no. But the one with the bag; boarding now, yes," I said. "Now he is loading a boat. Tomorrow he kills the president."

Twenty-two

We raced down to the pier, our feet skidding on the gang plank as the rain pelted down, but the boat was already pulling away. It kicked up a wake of rooster tails as it powered down the river, heading east towards the city.

Following these guys was our only chance to get to the heart of what was happening. We needed to give chase, and fast. I sprinted up to the main road and pulled my gun out on the first bike that I saw. Within moments I was gunning the throttle with Gina sat behind me, her arms wrapped around my waist.

We sped down to the embankment, me finding my rhythm in the ebb and flow of traffic, Gina keeping track of our assailants and shouting instructions and directions in my ear. Up ahead we could easily see the boat; the fastest moving thing on the water by a long way.

I was pushing the bike as hard as I could, but the rain and the traffic was making it difficult. No, not difficult. Dangerous. And, unlike the last time we were on a bike together, I had no prior knowledge of what was about to pull out on me.

The white line fever was real, the asphalt calling to me, urging me on, to ride faster, to throw caution to the wind as death no longer scared me, and a final end was a welcoming thought.

The squeeze of Gina around my waist as I took a corner at over seventy snapped me back to reality.

The bike was good. A newer BMW with fresh tyres, but I still felt the front slip a couple of times as I tried to find the river side roads with messenger bikes, busses, cars and pedestrians all venting at us as we carved them up, or nearly ran them over.

Some of this send my pulse racing even harder, some of it gave me a childlike thrill.

We tracked them all the way across the city, taking the river front roads where we could, and finding higher ground when we were forced to by the buildings.

A couple of times I thought I had lost them, but we could always see the wake it was leaving behind, and need just a glimpse of the distinctive red hull to know we were still in the chase.

I was watching the river as we came towards Vauxhall Bridge, and I just didn't see the taxi cab as he did a U-turn up ahead.

He was probably two or three hundred yards further up the road, and probably thought he had enough time.

I locked the front wheels up when I saw him moving into our path, the tyres skidding on the soaking wet road.

At the last minute, I saw him turn and see us. He away and put his arm up over his head as I tried to pull the bike around.

I managed to lean and turn, but we slammed sideways into the drivers' door.

I left the bike. I travelled up and over, but felt another weight push me down onto the roof of the taxi.

Gina.

Because we stole the bike, neither of us were wearing any helmets.

She cleared the cab and landed like a rag doll on the road in front of me.

She was sprawled out, face down, and not moving.

Me vision was blurred, and I braced myself to appear back in the Beast, or, actually, back in another taxi cab with Steph.

When nothing happened for a beat, I tried to move, but my torso was in agony. I had at least busted some ribs, and at worse, done some heavy internal damage.

I felt enormous relief that I had at least failed to leap back to a couple of days ago.

I also knew that in time, my little on-board nano support would attempt to fix me up, and I could already feel a burning on my left-hand side where it was at work.

I got onto all fours on the roof, and then up to a kneeling position. Gina still hadn't moved, and a crowd of onlookers were forming round us.

I scrambled off of the roof in a panic.

When I got to Gina, I had to push a couple of people out of the way that were standing over her, already trying turn her over.

Her left cheek was against the floor, and her eyes were closed. Her left arm was stuck underneath her body, and her legs were sprawled out behind her.

There was a trickle of blood coming out of her nose, and as I put my face close to hers, I couldn't detect any breathing.

I reached out a hand and put it to her cheek, and as I did, she groaned ever so slightly. The sense of relief was washing over me as she scrunched her eyelids together harder and let out another moan.

"Gina." She moaned again. "Gina. Are you hurt?" She opened one eye slightly, and tried to move. She winced as she picked her head up. "Mmmmm" was all she could manage.

"Gina. You need to tell me if you are OK."

She winced once more as she brough her right hand up under her body, and tried to push herself up. I hooked my arm under hers, and helped her to a stand.

She yelped as she moved her left arm. "Shit."

"What is it?"

"Your driving sucks, that's what."

She amazed me that she could try and crack a joke at a time like this. "Guilty," I said. "Are you in pain?"

She steadied herself and waved off my help. "Wrist. Possibly broken. Head hurts." She sucked in a lung full of air. "Ooh, yup. Ribs."

I held her forehead and put a finger in front of her eyes, moving it left and right. "Follow my finger." I pulled out a small light from my pocket and shone it in each of her eyes. "You most likely have mild concussion. Do you feel sick at all?"

"Er. Yup."

"Headache?"

"Yes."

"Well, there's nothing I can do right now."

"You really need to work on your bedside manner." She hobbled back towards the taxi, where the driver was climbing out of the passenger door. He stood up straight, rubbing the back of his neck.

When he saw us he picked up his pace. "Oh my god, are you guys alright? I never saw you coming."

Gina went around to the driver's door. "Sir, we need to borrow your cab."

Twenty-three

I was driving with Gina in the passenger compartment in the back.

This was a lot slower than the bike, and the steering wheel was vibrating quite a lot, most likely due to the damage to the front wheel caused by our accident.

The biggest problem was that we had now lost the boat.

We sped along past the MI5 building, and into Westminster. From there we carried on past London Bridge, and Tower Bridge until we came through to the other side of London, but still saw no signs of them.

"How much farther can we get?" said Gina from behind me. "They could be going all the way out to sea for all we know."

I pushed the cab even harder, the wheels complaining at my rough handling. "We keep going as far as we can until we see them – not many places to hide a bright red power boat on the river."

We were hitting the sections of the Thames where it starts to curve and snake. The traffic was getting lighter, so we were able to speed up even more.

We hit the river front and started scanning the water. I was weaving between the traffic whilst Gina had the binoculars trained on the Thames.

We were fast coming out of the centre of London, as I was worried that we had permanently lost sight of our target.

It was Gina who spotted them first. "There!" She opened the window and was zooming in. "Just saw a flash of red going round the bend. Couple of cargo boats blocking their path; must have slowed them a little."

And, sure enough, as we rounded the next corner of the river, we could see the distinctive red hull.

"Looks like they are slowing some more." I eased off at the same time and watched as Canary Warf came into view.

Very much the new financial district of London; London's Docklands emulated New York with its skyscrapers emblazoned with company logos of banks, tech and trading companies.

Where there weren't skyscrapers, there were bars and restaurants. And, even from across the river, the riverbank balconies of the hospitality industry were packed with people with drinks in hand, all sheltering under canopies as they laughed and joked the day away.

New money had recently come into the city in the form of green energy suppliers, and now that manufacturing of sustainable resources had become the new stock everyone in the city was after, they too were building at a fantastic rate.

Solar panels covered entire buildings, and the green of forest like gardens could be seen sprouting from the roof tops.

The power boat slowed and turned, headed for a small pier in front of a row of red brick warehouses on the north side of the river.

We ditched the now smoking cab and headed on foot to the pedestrian bridge that would take us over the water to where we could see the three men disembarking.

We didn't pass many people on the bridge, and we got to the other side to find ourselves in a much older, industrial feeling part of London.

We walked along the river front and approached the warehouse. A non-descript red brick building, three storeys high, it had a large open gate at the front, and small blue door on one side.

We crept around to the side and peered around the corner to watch the activity.

The three men were met by two others, and all of them exchanged hugs and handshakes as the bag was unloaded, and entered the warehouse via the large opening at the front.

The men disappeared inside, and we made our move. Gina's guns drawn, we stood either side of the blue door, and tried the handle. Locked.

Gina shook her head at me as I mimed shooting the door handle. We tracked around the back of the building, searching for another entrance, and spotted just what we needed. A fire escape ladder on the roadside of the warehouse snaked its way up the building. It looked old and creaky, but, more importantly, it was unguarded.

We cautiously climbed up until we reached the metal platform on the first floor. The door was locked, but the window next to it was cracked open for air, so I cupped my hands for Gina to climb up on. She put her foot in my palm, and I boosted her up. Once she was in, she reached down and hoisted me in.

I got to my feet and surveyed the scene. We were on a gantry that ran along the internal perimeter of the building, which was one large open space floor.

A table was set in the centre, and four out of the five men we saw were sitting around it, setting up a game of cards. They were all lost in their game as I took my binoculars and got a closer look at their faces. The Korean security agent was there, along with two other Korean nationals. The fourth man was a Caucasian, possibly European or American; hard to tell – but he seemed to be the ringleader in the game, dealing out each hand and generally talking the most.

I scanned across the floor to an office at the far end. The angle I was at meant that I could only see the legs of the people moving around, but a counted at least three more.

A couple of them moved toward the window, and I could see them more clearly.

There, only twenty feet from our location, was the face I had been seeing every day since this began.

Gim.

He was talking to another man, waving his arms and pointing at the bag that I had seen in the boat earlier. The man he was talking to placed the bag on the floor, unzipped it and very slowly and carefully took out a metal unit with an aerial sticking out of the side, and a mobile phone strapped to the top. He gingerly put it on the table, and wiped the sweat off his palms on the top of his trousers.

It had a few wires coming out from the base of the phone, with a few left hanging with plugs on the end. The whole thing was about the size of a shoe box, and was held together with odd-sized screws. The metal casing looked mismatched on either side, and I could see a couple of gaps at the joins.

I recognised this type of device from my time serving in the forces. I had seen many of these types of things on the roadside, or strapped to an oil drum or the underside of a truck and left parked next to the army barracks. It was designed to trigger a bomb. It was a detonator.

I slowly went to pass the binoculars towards Gina, but as I pulled them down from my eyes, the sensation of vertigo came over me again. It felt like I was on a boat, and we were capsizing, about to be thrown into the sea. I stared on a fixed point in front of me with all my might, willing my mind to settle, showing my brain that we weren't moving; trying to recalibrate.

Not now, I thought. *Of all times, not now.*

I stumbled backwards, reacting but at the same time trying not to make a sound. I thrust out my hand, and grabbed hold of the railings in front of me. A second wave came over me and the room spun as I gripped tighter on the metal bar.

I could feel my palms clamming, and beads of sweat breaking out on my brow. A pain in my chest made my headache worse, and I let go of the railings to wipe my brow.

At that moment, I felt something slip from my grip. In a moment of panic my eyes sprang open to see the binoculars sliding from my hand. They bounced once on the edge of the gantry, and, as if in slow motion, toppled toward the edge. They stopped just before reaching the precipice, and came to a rest, balancing on the point of falling.

Gina's arm was already reaching for them, but I was closer. We both moved to grab them but got in each other's way. All Gina's hand served to do was to knock mine out of the way, and between us, we fumbled against the binoculars, and punted them towards the edge.

They stopped, half over the edge, and half still on safe ground.

They were rocking back and forth, teasing us with the idea of falling. I put my hand on the floor to steady myself. I felt the vibration through the gantry as I did, and watched as that final move sent them spinning towards the floor below.

They tumbled in slow motion, pitching and yawing as they tumbled down, down, down and got smaller and smaller as they fell. They smashed against the concrete floor with a splintering bang. The resultant sound echoed around the room like gunfire, making all of the men below us instinctively duck their heads and cover their ears as the sound of a small, innocent pair of binoculars exploded around the warehouse like a firework in a tin can. We leapt to our feet and made for the far wall, as shouts from the men boomed up at us, the office below spilling out more men than I had counted.

There was one door in front of us, and, thankfully it was open. We raced along the gantry and flew inside, the door thick and heavy, and slammed it behind us as the sound of footsteps on the metal stairs came racing up behind us.

The room we found ourselves in was dimly lit, but we could see enough to be able to slide the large bolt across the door, just as the banging and thumping on the other side told us they were only inches away on the other side.

This room was completely different to the rest of the warehouse. It was cladded in grey foam in panels suspended from the walls and ceilings, and as soon as we had shut the door, the men's shouts became muffled and distant.

I located a switch next to the door and flipped it.

Lights and power came on to reveal a small room with a desk in front of us. It had a computer terminal, and a sound mixing desk with a loom of wires running out and across the room. In front of the desk were lights on stands – the kind you see on a film set, and a camera set up pointing at the far wall.

The wall itself was a free-standing structure – possibly made of slabs of breeze block to make it look more like the inside of a cave than the inside of a television studio – covered in a grey cloth, with the symbol of the Hwarang, and a chair was set up in front. Two microphones were suspended above, and a large white board was set up facing the chair.

I recognised the scene immediately. I had seen it on the big screen at Buckingham Palace countless times, but it was still eerie to see it in the flesh.

Even though I had grown accustomed to the sense of déjà vu, this still sent a chill running up and down my spine.

I had found it.

By sheer dumb luck, but I had found it.

As I walked around to the board, it was covered in marker pen notes of what Gim would say to camera. I stood and took it all in.

"What is all this?" Gina asked.

I was scanning all of the detail of the room, matching it up to my memories of the scenes outside Buckingham Palace. "This is where Gim is filming from tomorrow."

Gina was studying the camera, and walked over and looked at the computer terminal. "Looks like it's all powered up."

The banging and shouting outside the door had stopped. "That door is reinforced, but they will get through. Check to see if there is a rear entrance," said Gina as she studied the equipment.

As Gina played with the controls, I checked out the rear. Nothing but four walls. Trapped. Like rats in a maze for the second time in one day.

A bang reverberated outside. A bullet-shaped dent bulged out from the door on our side. More shouting and thumping.

I came back to Gina. "Nothing. The only way out is the way in."

She was studying the screen. "OK, I have something here. See if you can turn that camera on." She pointed over towards the tripod and I went over and found the power.

"Done." I watched what she was doing as another sound started up outside. This time a whirring motor. "We don't have much time. What are you thinking?"

"We are off grid – no phones – but we can send a broadcast out using this equipment." She looked up from what she was doing. "We can send a warning to the world from here."

She paused and looked at me like I was supposed to understand. I shrugged my shoulders at her. She rolled her eyes and pointed. "Get on the chair and I'll start the broadcast."

I looked at the small seat like it was an executioner's chair. And, perhaps, in some sort of macabre way, it was.

I walked my own personal green mile and sat down. "What do I say?"

"Anything that comes to mind. Tell the world what we know. Where we are."

"The world?" She pushed a button.

"We are live. Go."

"What?" I said as a red light came on the camera. I cleared my throat and looked down the lens.

"Hello." A shrill grinding sound started up from outside. I jumped at the noise.

I cleared my throat once more. "Hello. My name is Doctor Gibson Hill, and I am with the US Secret Service. If anyone is watching this, I am talking to you from a warehouse on the north side of London's Docklands. We have tracked the terrorist know as 'Gim' to this location and, right now, he and his associates are trying to cut through the door between us and them. They will break through in a matter of minutes, and will most likely kill us."

The grinding sound had stopped, and was replaced by a rumble. A drill.

"We have uncovered a plot to trigger a series of explosions at Battersea Nuclear Power Station, and use sleeper cell agents to create terror and panic in London at the moment of President McDonald's speech outside the gates of Buckingham Palace, tomorrow, at the NATO summit, at just after noon."

A heavy series of thumps was coming through the door.

"I make this recording in the hope that this plot can be stopped in time, and save millions of lives." I paused, not knowing what else to say.

The door had fallen silent. I realised what was missing. The warning I had put in place over and over again had fallen on deaf ears. The problem ran deeper now; I realised that.

"But we have discovered that this runs deep in my own government. I do not know who to trust, and who is an ally. All I know is that the president will start a speech tomorrow, and never make it to the end."

Sweat was forming on my brow. I looked up at Gina, who was gesturing for me to continue.

"If anyone is out there…" I trailed off.

The door burst open, and the men, fully armed, all streamed in, guns blazing.

Twenty-four

We dived for cover behind the desk, just as the door was kicked down and shards of wood exploded from the front and top.

The furniture shook and holes appeared about three or four centimetres wide; dirt, splinters and light smashed through as our fragile cover began to disintegrate.

Gina and I were lying flat on the floor, our stomachs clenched against the dusty ground. We were being hammered. The desk lurched as its structure started to break down. Gina looked sideways at me as she slid her gun out from underneath her and directed it to my temple.

I shook my head, something inside me knew I wouldn't survive another trip back.

There was a pause in the gunfire for a moment as the click and snap of metal permeated the air.

Reloading.

Gina whispered "Wall. Now!" as she sprang to her feet. She turned in the air and fired blindly behind her as she ran backwards to the far side of the wall.

The men had reloaded and started firing back. Gina ducked her head as the cloth danced under the impact of the firefight.

She fell backwards; her gun out in front, pumping the trigger with deadly aim. She pushed her feet down into the ground and slid herself backwards in her bottom to the wall.

At the same time, I turned around and got into a crouching position so I could peer around the sides.

Gina was reloading. I kept my head low, and snuck a glance at the scene. One man had taken a bullet in the neck, blood spurting from his mouth as he collapsed to his knees.

Another was holding his shoulder, and the others had dropped back into the doorway for cover.

I turned back to the wall to see nothing but small holes in the breeze block.

The silence was broken by a man by the doorway. "We know you are in there, Doctor Hill." The voice was unmistakable, having heard it multiple times on the screens above Buckingham Palace.

"Why don't you come out, and we can settle this without any more bloodshed."

I was sitting on the floor; my back to the wall. My only protection. And Gina had the only gun. The game was up.

"You plan to kill millions, Gim. You don't care about bloodshed." My head was throbbing. I no longer cared if I lived or died. I had had enough.

"Maybe so, but I am fighting for a cause. A cause to stop the real terrorist. The one who risk the security of millions of my countrymen. What do you fight for, American?"

I was scanning around the room, still looking for any way out. But it was futile.

The walls behind us were just that – walls with no windows or doors. All sealed up to prevent unwanted light and prying eyes peeking through.

Surely that contravened some kind of buildings regulations? Must complain to the landlord when I get out of this.

I was tired.

"Killing innocents isn't just, or noble. It's cowardly."

Was that sirens in the distance?

"You have exactly one minute to come out, or we will shoot you where you lie." I laughed. Laughed out loud. The first time I had let out a laugh like that in days. Or this day.

"What is it with you and a countdown, Gim?"

I was still scanning the walls and ceiling around me. There were no windows or doors, and all of the walls looked smooth. No hidden exits.

Above my head was a loom of cables that ran the length of the room. They started at various points over on the far wall, and fed power to all of the gear in the room. They bundled together and snaked their way overhead until they

155

reached the junction box by the doorway. Next to the door was a fuse box that ran a coil of wires out of door and down into the main warehouse.

The sirens were definitely getting louder. But this was a major city. They could be going anywhere.

Gina reappeared around the side of the wall and fired. She got off two shots as the men instantly fired back.

I heard the click as she pulled the trigger the third time, and a mark of blood was left on the cloth.

"Out of ammo, honey."

My head was spinning again. All I wanted was for this nightmare to end.

Gina appeared around the wall once more. From my position, I could just see the edge of her shoulder as she reached into her pocket for another clip.

She was struggling with her injured wrist from the bike fall earlier, and now it looked as though the whole arm was out of action, as blood was seeping onto the sleeve of her shirt.

She reloaded her final clip and locked eyes on me.

I started to mouth to her *Fuse box*.

She squinted and cocked her head slightly. She couldn't understand me.

I tried again. This time eve more elaborate mouth movements. *F-u-s-e-b-o-x*.

She pursed her lips and grimaced.

I had to think quickly.

"Thirty seconds, Doctor Hill," came the voice of Gim. "I am a busy man, and I don't have time to waste. Thirty seconds to come out. Then we take you out."

My head cleared slightly. A thought appeared for a fleeting moment that I grabbed hold of before it disappeared like a dream just after you wake.

"OK. OK I'm coming out."

Gina shot me a glance again. This time her eyes were saying no.

"I slowly raised my hands above my head. "I'm going to stand up slowly and turn and face you."

I tucked my feet closer, ready to stand.

"I know you have the power, so I am at your mercy."

I shifted onto my haunches. "I am unarmed. Like I said you have all of the power here. I am at your mercy. I have no power." I looked earnestly at Gina who was shaking her head.

"Please, don't get angry, don't blow a *fuse*." I winced as I said that last part.

But Gina snapped her head up and started scanning the room. I moved cautiously around to face them.

I had my hands above my head; palms facing out.

"That's better," said a voice from behind the doorway. I could only see a silhouette, but it was Gim. He stepped forward into the light.

"Now. On your knees."

I dropped to one knee, and then the other.

"Good. Now link your hands behind your head. Slowly." He was very calm and measured. All guns were trained on me.

All of the gunmen looked up and to my right and Gina appeared from behind the wall and took a supportive stance.

She fired two, three shots into the heart of the fuse box, and dropped back behind her cover as it exploded with a white heat, sparks and flame. The gunmen reacted and looked to their side as they cowered away.

Lights went out and all of the equipment went off behind and in front of me.

With no windows in the room, we were plunged into darkness.

All of the men we were attacking were silhouetted against the door with the little daylight there was coming in, but we were dark to them, so as Gina squeezed off as many rounds as she could, I dived behind her for cover.

She hit the water pipe next to the fuse box, and that sent a high-pressure spray of water across the doorway, shocking the men into pausing, ducking, buying me valuable seconds.

The return fire had already come. I ducked behind a cabinet in the corner in the room as bullets ricocheted off the walls next to me.

How many were left? Had she hit anyone?

The answer came quickly.

"Hill!" screamed Gim. "If you do not stop this now, I will put a bullet in her brain!"

I peeked around the side of the cabinet. The scene was grim. She had hit three of the eight men in the warehouse. One more was lying on the ground holding a bleeding leg. The rest of the floor and doorway was covered in bodies. Water still spraying out of the pipe.

Just next to the wall, but forward of it was Gina. She was on her knees, blood soaking the side of her shirt. Standing above her, with gun pointing at her head was Gim.

"Come out. Now."

I tried to think of a way out, another option, my brain was scrambled. I had no other options. I was out of them. Once again, I came out with my hands above my head.

"What did you send?" Gim said, pointing at the camera.

I was silent. Stalling for time.

Gim cocked his gun and shot Gina in the calf. She screamed and fell to the floor. He grabbed her by the hair and pulled her back up. She was pale. Shaking.

"Once again. What did you send?"

"We recorded a message. Told the world of your plans."

Gim pointed to one of the remaining men behind him. "Put her in the chair."

He came over and grabbed Gina, and dragged her over to the chair in front of the camera. He put on a pig mask that was laying on the floor nearby, and used some rope to tie her down.

Gim stood behind her, and the other man stood in front of me, gun trained on my head.

"Get the power back on."

One of the men started pulling wires out of the fuse box, and swore as sparks came out of the junction.

He made a few more attempts at rewiring sections that had burnt out, and, after a while, the camera lights came back on. "Only lights had been fused. Everything else still functional," said the man at the fuse box.

"Good. Then we shall begin."

The man went over to the camera and switched it on.

"Tie him to the table." Gim directed to the man with the gun trained on me. "Facing me. I want him to see this."

I was roughly grabbed and thrown to the floor facing Gim. My hands were tied behind me, and through the table leg.

The other man in the room donned a pig mask, and took a position next to his comrade either side of Gim; their guns held pointing up in defiance.

I tugged on my restraints, but they were not giving any slack. I gave it one hard yank, and the table shook, and a roll of tape hit the floor.

Gim started his piece to camera. "McDonald!" His face was crimson, and spit flew from his mouth as he spoke. "You have failed to stop me! And now I have one of your own. We have been triumphant, and soon, you we see that we do not show mercy to the Americans!"

He reached behind his back and pulled out a knife. A long blade with one side smooth, one side serrated.

"I have a number of requests," he continued. "But first, to demonstrate my seriousness, I shall take something from you."

He grabbed Gina by the hair, and put the knife to her throat.

I thrashed and kicked, but my bonds were too strong. I watched at Gim slowly drew the blade across, leaving I raw line of blood as it went. Not deep enough to kill, but enough to cause pain.

Gina was hyperventilating. "McDonald. Every three minutes that go by where you don't talk to me directly, I make another cut. Each one deeper than the last. I will slice through her delicate neck one slither at a time." He looked at his watch. "The first three minutes has started."

"Gim, please." I couldn't just sit there idle, I had to try something. Anything. "The US does not negotiate. He will not call you, or meet you, or talk to you. You are wasting your time."

He pointed the blood-stained knife at me. "You. You are next on my list. If I kill her, you will take her place."

"Then take me now." Gina was shaking her head at me. "Take me instead of her. Let her go. A show of good faith will go a long way." I paused as my mind raced. "Do it for the Lynx." I had no idea what I had just said, but it had an effect.

"You do not speak that name! You have not earned the honour!" He looked at his watch. "You see, McDonald! Your agents try to negotiate! This is what happens!" He took the knife once more, and, teeth clenched, drew it again across Gina's neck. Both henchmen having to hold her head as she thrashed and screamed.

"Gim! Wait!" I was clutching at straws now. I had nothing left to lose. "I know of the honour. I too have fought and lost. You would be dishonouring me if you do not let me take her place in that chair. I know of the plot at Battersea, I know of the media helicopter you plan to bring down tomorrow."

Gim marched over to me and crouched down, our faces close. "How do you know? Why don't I just kill you now?"

"Because I have died a hundred times already." Gim contemplated me for a moment.

"Not like this, my friend." Gim took his knife and cut my ropes, then hauled my up on my feet and dragged me over behind Gina. The two henchmen placed their guns on the floor, and held me firm against the wall.

"McDonald! Your agent tries to beg like a coward! We show no mercy to cowards!"

He stood behind me, grabbed my hair and slashed the knife with force across my neck and dumped it on the floor. The pain exploded like a hot wave, and I could feel the warm blood cascading down my neck as I was let go and crumpled to the floor.

My vision was closing in, a corona of dark was collapsing into my view as I became light headed, and rolled on my back.

I knew this feeling. It the feeling of adrenaline coursing through my veins. My body pumping everything it had into my bloodstream to get me to take action.

My heart was slowing down. A warmth was spreading over me like a comforting wave, and I felt relaxed.

I closed my eyes and waited.

My thought wandered to my childhood. Long summers playing with the sprinklers in the garden, my mother and father watching from chairs reclined on the decking.

My sister playing alongside me without a care in the world, laughing and screaming with delight as the cool water hit us as we ran through. The smell of the lawn.

The wave of nostalgia that passed over me was kicked into touch by another wave of adrenaline.

Not now. Can't you see I just want to go to sleep.

Then the burning in my neck grew hotter and hotter, the pain cutting through my misery like a hot knife, the tingling turning to a fire; an itch like a thousand tiny insects scratching and biting across my windpipe.

I was so used to being thrown back to the rear seat of the Beast, that I forgotten what dying really felt like.

But I was still here.

I opened my eyes. I could see a lot of blood on the floor. My blood. I stared at the ceiling for a moment, and my vision cleared a little. The burning in my neck was still there. Fierce, penetrating. But something else had replaced it. Another feeling. Another sensation.

Rage.

I slowly brought my hand up to my throat. It was slick with blood, but the wound had knitted back together.

I rolled my head to the side. Gim was standing behind Gina. Both henchmen were back at his side, guns raised. Then I saw something glisten behind Gim's feet.

The knife.

Gim was speaking again. "Another three minutes are up, McDonald! This one she may not sur—"

I moved my hand to grab the knife. My head was behind one of the gunman's feet. I rallied myself, and lunged forward and grabbed the handle. I slashed the back of the gunman's right ankle with the blade. He screamed, and just as I planned, fell backward across me. As he did, I wrapped my hand around him and turned, just as the other gunman wheeled around. I pulled the trigger.

The semi-automatic sent the man flying backwards, as I took the knife and drove it into the chest of the man on top of me.

Gim went for the gun now lying on the floor, but I aimed and shot him in the legs.

I quickly got up from under the now dead henchman and shot the stunned camera operator squarely in the chest.

Gim was crawling for the gun, but I was on him in seconds. I grabbed him by the hair and dragged him back in front of camera.

I dumped him in a sitting position on the floor, and cut the ropes tying up Gina. She stood and marched over to the gun Gim was crawling towards moments ago.

With blood dripping from her wounds, she pushed the muzzle roughly against his temple. "Give me one reason. Just one."

Gim spat on the floor. "I will be a martyr to my people. The warriors are ready. You have no idea what you will cause."

I stepped between them. "This is Special Agent Hill, of the US Secret Service. We are in control of the situation."

I took the gun and shot Gim squarely between the eyes. "Mission accomplished."

***

I could hear the squadron downstairs, as officers moved into the building and made a systematic search as they worked their way up to us.

Myself and Gina were still in the camera room; both of us were slumped against the wall exhausted.

The team entered the room and fanned out. They checked the bodies and swept for explosives as they signalled the rest to join them.

"Agent Hill?" said the squadron leader, as he entered the room, gun trained on us.

"Yes, sir," was all I could muster. I had felt better, but also a lot worse. I looked over at the seat as Gina was being helped to her feet by another officer.

More people had entered the room, and I could see men in suits looking around. When they saw me, Li and Salanski came over.

"That was reckless, Agent Hill. Going rouge like that."

I was struggling to talk, the pain in my head worsening. "Yes sir, I know, sir. I had an opportunity—"

He slapped me on the side of the arm. "We'll sort this out back at base. Your video is all over the internet. Caused quite a diplomatic storm." He tipped down his shades and winked. "But glad you're OK."

"Me too, sir."

Another man came over to me and introduced himself.

"Detective Gould, MI6. We need you to come with us and give us a full debrief, Doctor Hill."

I tried to sit up straighter. Gina was in the corner having the wound on her shoulder dressed.

"We have been tracking Gim in Europe for some time now. We have been waiting for him to strike. I understand you have some insider knowledge as to the next planned attack?"

I tried to clear my head, but the throbbing was getting worse. "Yes, sir. They planned to blow up Battersea Nuclear Power Station. Also, a string of operatives in the UK set to cause anarchy in the crowds at Buckingham Palace at the NATO summit speeches."

Gould was making notes on his tablet as he spoke. "Fortunately, you spooked the group at the power station before they had a chance to set the explosives fully. We have a team there now working with officials and the bomb squad to make it safe."

The relief washed over me like a warm blanket. We had done it. We had stopped the bomb.

"Unfortunately," Gould continued, "they now know we are on to them, and have switched to an alternative plan."

That cleared my head like a cold shower. Gould had my phone in his hands, and he showed me the screen.

"Where do you get this from?" His tone had changed. On the screen was the app the security guard at the power station had downloaded. The room at fallen silent as eyes were turning to us.

"The guard at Battersea is one of them. We convinced him we were anti-McDonald and he put it on there. It's been dormant since this morning when we spoke to him."

"Well, now it's not."

On the screen was a single message:

The flower has lost its petal, but the stem is still strong. The shape had changed. Tomorrow they will know our name. The Lynx is still strong.

I took the phone for a closer look. "What does that mean?"

Gould put his tablet away. "We believe that Gim was not the leader. More of a puppet, and that this 'Lynx' person is still at large."

"And the rest of the message? *The shape has changed*?"

Gould sighed as he rubbed his temples. "They are reverting to plan B."

"Plan B?"

"Yes, and unless we can find out who this Lynx person is, you just killed our only source."

My head was spinning again. Worse than before at the hotel. It felt as though the ground was moving, even though my eyes told me it wasn't.

"Any bright ideas?" A group of MI6 operatives had crowded around us, along with Salanski and Li. All were waiting on my next response.

I blacked out.

Twenty-five

It was late into the night the day before the summit, and we had been up for hours in the operations room at Winfield House, trying to figure out our next move.

Salanski was in the seat next to me, and was cradling a paper coffee cup like his life depended on it; which wasn't so far from the truth.

All except Li had removed their ties and jackets, and were in varying states of falling asleep or just slumped across their chairs.

Li was always impeccably dressed. He didn't seem to look tired, either, still throwing out ideas and theories to analysts that were stifling yawns and rubbing their reddening eyes.

The wind was blowing leaves, branches and debris across the lawn. Small urban wildlife was scampering for cover and the rain continued raging against the window outside. It had been cracked open to let in some fresh air to keep us awake, but along with the air came the noise of the city.

I was driving myself crazy convincing myself that I could predict the rise and fall of the hubbub of traffic, people and late-night creatures like a movie I had seen countless time before. But this was, of course, not true. We had not yet reached the moment in the motorcade where I would reset countless times. The sense of déjà vu that I had been experiencing over the last day was dominant in my perception of the world. I was aware that I was overanalysing everything, and questioning what had changed, and how I had changed it.

What would happen when I reached that moment back in the motorcade? Would I sail on through? Or disappear into nothing as the universe decided *you have had enough now, sonny. Time to give it up.*

I was all out of ideas, and starting to wish I could just choose to jump off this treadmill.

No way out for you, sonny. I could hear the universe mocking me. *You're on this gravy train for ever now. Strap in and enjoy the ride.*

In my head, the universe now had claws, and a huge grin and red eyes, beckoning me towards him like the devil who lay in wait at the end of my journey.

Jeez. Need to snap out if this funk I'm in.

I stood up and walked over to the window. The rain was still lashing down, and the purple clouds suggested no let up until all this was over.

What have I done? Have I damaged something, perhaps irreversibly?

The analysts at the front of the room were looking like a bunch of students after a long night out. Except the night was still young, and sleep was not one of our luxuries.

What is it about these guys and hoodies? My thoughts were wandering. I could feel the pull of fatigue as my mind began to shut down.

Is it standard issue to wear one, just like the black suits for us guys? Do they pull you aside at some point in your training and show you a picture of some tech company boss – the ones out in California – and say 'This is what you're aiming for, guys. Hipster nerd.'

I need to sleep.

No, I need coffee. I stepped out of the room and headed down the corridor. People were still milling about, but it was at a much slower pace than this morning (whatever that meant).

As I entered the kitchen to find the coffee machine, Joel was standing there on his phone. He jumped as he saw me.

"Sorry. Didn't mean to scare you, Thomas."

He pocketed his handset and grabbed the coffee pot. "No worries – just a bit jumpy. Here's to too much caffeine," he said as he raised the pot in salute.

"I hear ya, buddy. Load me up." He poured me a cup and handed it to me.

He seemed sluggish, and stared at the floor as he let the drink swirl around his cup.

"Say, any luck with the app on my phone yet?" The coffee had been sitting in the pot for a while, and had started to go cold, but I was grateful, nonetheless for the drink.

"No, not yet. Very complex thing." He went over to refill his cup and pointed at my mug.

"No, I'm good. Thanks."

I badly needed to grab some sleep. But the risk of missing something was too great. What if something happened as I was dozing? This could be my only chance at solving this, and I couldn't be caught napping. Literally. No, I would tough it out till the end. Then figure out how to get this nano out of me without killing me, or worse, sending me back to the cab a day ago and resetting everything we had done. Forget about my body; I don't think my mind could take it.

I resolved to carry on. I made to go back to the operations room and figure this out. I looked at the hoodie in front of me. "Right, let's see if we can crack this app. Find the source."

He saluted his coffee cup once more. "Yep. Be there in a sec."

I headed back to the operations room.

It felt like the mood had darkened still since I left to grab a drink. Heads had lowered and eyes were blinking hard.

The ambient glow of the monitors was the bathing the room in an eerie electronic hue.

My phone had been plugged into the console for most of the evening, with most of the team trying to hack into the software to no avail.

The *EnkripChat* was open, and they were trying to find the source of the messages.

"OK," said Li, causing most of the room to jump at the noise. "Can we honey trap them in some way into sending a message?" He was addressing the room in general as Joel sat back down at his terminal.

"What do you have in mind?" Gina was also clutching a cup of black nectar, and had a ring of dark circles under her eyes.

There is only so much coffee that we can all take.

Li waved his hands in the air. "I dunno, maybe, uh. We could put out a statement to the press. Let them know we are onto them."

"And risk a sudden attack? No way. Too risky." Gina was pacing the room. She walked over to Li and patted him on the shoulder. "But good idea. I'm glad you're thinking."

I sat down in a chair near the back of the room. The sound of typing had stopped, and the only noise was the rain hitting the window outside.

Solving a crime isn't as glamourous as I thought it would be. I smiled to myself.

A buzzing sound broke the silence.

Office chairs bounced as several of the team sprang out of their seats. "App is active." Li was over to my phone first. "Incoming message."

The room instantly started buzzing. "Put it up on screen," ordered Gina.

The app from my phone was displayed above.

Converge on the target at 1000 hrs for the attack.

I took a moment to process the meaning. "Must be Buckingham Palace in the morning. They plan to converge en masse." I had long since stopped trying to hide my foreknowledge.

"Joel, trace the signal." I felt relief that this could be finally over.

My hooded college spoke. "Not possible. App is too sophisticated."

My frustration was boiling over. "But what about the meta data imbedded in the message? Isn't it a fact that it exists to help stop terror attacks? Should be a piece of cake, right?"

I was searching Joel's eyes for an answer.

"Sorry, no. Just isn't possible." He turned back to his terminal.

One of the other analysts next to his span in his chair. "No, he's right. Why didn't we think of that before? Just break into the tags in the background and we can get a location ping." He scooted over to Joel's terminal and went to start typing. Joel batting him away.

"No, Des, it won't work."

Des gave a puzzled look. "Yes, yes it will. Just open the message and…"

Joel pulled his keyboard away. "No, it isn't possible, now carry on with the social media scanning."

Li shrugged his shoulders at me. "Just leave 'em. They know what they are doing."

I went over to Gina and leant into her ear. "This is wrong. Joel definitely said he could use the metadata in the app, and it would be a piece of cake as long as he had a message come through."

Joel had left his desk again, so I went up to Des and spoke to him. "Hey, Des. Do me a favour. Test my idea. Don't worry, you won't get into trouble."

Des looked over towards the door as he moved over to Joel's terminal. He brought up the screen that showed the app, and the message we just received.

"There. Look." He pointed at a series of numbers on screen.

"What am I looking at?" I asked.

"This is the trace that shows the location of where the message was sent from." He copied the data into another section of his screen and punched a few buttons.

He rubbed his face as he looked around the room.

"What? What is it?"

"The signal is bounced through a couple of servers globally, but… no, hang on… let me try again." He repeated the exercise, and when he finished, grabbed tuft-fulls of hair and vigorously rubbed his scalp.

"What is it, Des?" He was still rubbing his head, as if the self-massage would somehow soften the blow of the bad thoughts he was now experiencing.

"Something's wrong. It didn't work."

"Why? What happened?"

"Says it's coming from inside."

"Inside? What, inside…?"

"Inside here. Within five metres of us, in fact."

I straightened up and scanned the room. In the service you got good and spotting people who were guilty, or about to do something. You could spot the nervous ones, the distracted ones, the ones who were focussed on something different to the crowd.

No one seemed to fit the profile.

"Another message coming through." Joel had grabbed the phone and was pulling it up for us to see.

New target. Home base. Immediate.

Des was typing frantically. "Coming from this building again."

"Where's Joel?" I was scanning the room for the senior analyst.

"Kitchen?" Gina and Li followed me as we went back down the corridor.

Nothing was in the kitchen apart from the coffee pot.

"Somebody call him." Gina dialled his number. We could hear a vibrating noise straight away. It was nearby.

We started looking around the room. Using our ears to guide us, we all converged near the drinks station as the buzzing stopped.

"Dial it again."

I moved my hand over the coffee, and then under where there was a cabinet, and a waste bin.

I pulled out the drawer housing the rubbish and the buzzing instantly grew louder.

I yanked the bin bag out and tipped it over the floor. Amongst the cartons and chocolate bar wrappers was a phone. I picked it up. "Is that Thomas's?" I couldn't tell, but Gina dialled it again and it buzzed in my hand with her name on the display.

"Where is he?"

Gina was on her radio already "All agents, secure the building. Analyst Joel Thomas has gone AWOL. Repeat. Do not let him leave the building."

The alarm was sounding as Li checked his firearm. "Any ideas what the message means?" He asked as we walked back towards the operations room.

"The latest text on the app? No, but it sounds like something is going to happen now."

I wished I hadn't spoken. As from outside came an all too familiar cry.

"Aelililililil!"

"Aelililililil!"

"Aelililililil!"

Li and Gina stopped and looked around. "What in the name of God is that?"

I was still moving towards the operations room. "An attack from the guerrillas. Was set for tomorrow. Looks like the timeline got brought forward."

I located Des and gave him Joel's phone. "Can you break into it?"

Des took it and connected it to his computer. "Maybe. Gonna take some time."

I slapped him on the shoulder. "For once it's something I don't have."

"Ma'am?" Salanski was standing next to us with his tie undone, hair unkempt and a smell of stale coffee coming from his breath. He also was drawing his firearm. "A mob is forming outside. They are trying to come over the fence."

"OK, listen up everyone." The activity stopped as all eyes fell to her. She stood firm, her posture strong, her eyes clear. "We have an unknown number of hostiles trying to storm the building. Priority is protecting the first family who are upstairs. POTUS and VP will be informed but are off site. We need to contain and protect. Shoot to wound only. Agent Li. Inform the British Service that we require assistance. Agent Salanski. You are team lead on the snipers. Rooftop shooters to fire warning shots only at this stage. Do we have tear gas?"

"Yes, ma'am. Launchers on the roof will be on standby."

"OK, team. You know your roles. Hill, you are with me. Can someone arm him? Li, join us out front once you have called the Brits."

"Ma'am."

She paused as she surveyed the room. "And call the press. Let them know what is happening. Get them down here."

"Ma'am?" Li had his phone in hand, but had stopped dialling. "The press?"

"How do you stop an enemy who are attacking you? How do you stop an aggressor who wants to tear you down, impose their view on you? Someone who wants to turn the world against you and run you out of town?"

I smirked at this. She may have been awake for what felt like days now, but I could see why she rose to the top so quickly.

"You let the world see what they really are."

Salanski holstered his gun and made for the stairs.

"Now can someone furnish Doctor Hill with a weapon?"

***

Outside, the weather was intensifying. The wind was pushing the rain across in waves like a fog across the perfectly manicured lawn.

I was standing at an angle just to stay upright, and my raincoat was doing little to stop freezing damp penetrating my very bones.

Across the lawn were a row of trees and hedges, and I knew that behind those was a twelve-foot-tall cast iron fence with barbs along the top.

I squinted through the rain to see if there was any movement up ahead, but the night shielded the attackers from view.

I could just make out a noise in the distance. Not the war cry of earlier, but a screeching, screaming sound.

172

"What is that?" Gina was shining a torch over towards the trees.

"Look," I said. "Is that a light?" A yellowish glow was flickering in the distance, but was too erratic for torchlight.

"They're cutting the fence." She spoke into her radio once more. "All eyes on the far side of the lawn; hostiles are cutting through the perimeter."

The grinding, screeching sound had stopped. All we could hear was the wind.

Then it came once more.

"Aelilililililil!"

"All agents. Here they come."

A flicker of light appeared behind the trees, then a beam, quickly followed by more that bobbed up and down.

"Tear gas canisters ready," ordered Gina. "Hold until my mark."

Then they appeared. I was not quite ready for the sight. So much so that I took an involuntary step backwards.

Ten, then twenty, then more pig-masked people stampeded towards us waving baseball bats, clubs, machetes and chains. Feet splashing in the mud below them, all charging straight for us.

"Fire gas," said Gina as we both retreated back into the relative safety of the building.

I heard the dull pressure of the canisters being fired, and turned to see them bouncing in front of the angry mob. But they had little effect. The wind was so strong, it carried most of it away. Some poor soul half a mile down the road would get tear gassed.

We made it into the house and pulled the reinforced glass doors shut behind us, just as the first of the attackers reached the outside.

The anger was frightening.

All of the pigs were pounding on the glass. The ones with weapons were at the front, and slamming the doors with what they had to hand, but the structure was holding. For now.

"I hope this is reinforced?" I say, as much to myself as Gina.

"Designed to withstand bullets and heavy arms fire. Should keep them out for a while."

Other agents had appeared at our side. All taking a stance with their guns drawn.

Behind the mob, more lights appeared. This time much more powerful, brighter searchlights.

Salanski came over the radio. "Ma'am. Drones are approaching. Readying snipers on your command."

A swarm of them circled around the grounds, moving at speed behind the mob, and circling the roof.

"Negative, snipers. Do not engage."

"Ma'am? They are coming in at close range."

"Are they armed?"

"Ma'am?"

"Repeat. Do they have weapons capabilities?"

"Unknown, ma'am, visibility is extremely poor."

"Do not fire unless fired upon. That is an order. We cannot shoot into the sky and risk a miss in a large city. Bullets could hit anything out there."

"What had that one got?" Li was beside us, and pointing at the door. "It's a pickaxe of some kind."

A large man in the same mask was swinging heavily at the glass. At first, I wasn't worried, but as he swung more and more, I could see a chip forming where he struck.

"Li, ETA on backup?"

"British command sending units as we speak."

The man continued swinging his pickaxe. His aim was good, but he hit in slightly different spot each time, leaving and series of pock marks on the glazing.

Over time, the repetition had built up, and a star shaped splinter in the glass had formed.

He swung again and hit just to the side. His arms were forming smaller arcs as he tired, but the odds of him striking the same spot were improving with each swing.

He hit dead centre of the weakened point on the next attempt, and there was a sound like ice cracking as a small dribble of rain water made its way through to the inside of the glass.

He swung once more and the splinter turned into a crack, and the agents clocked their guns.

"Shoot to wound only, gentlemen. Shoot to wound."

On the next hit the window gave. A shattering sound of the glass smashing to the ground let the wind and rain slam its way in as stampeding feet and a rising war cry charged us.

Guns all fired at the same time. I shot blindly at the floor, aiming for feet and legs as some of the men fell. We were overwhelmed by the numbers.

"Retreat and lock doors!" ordered Gina as we fell back into the operations room. We slammed the heavy doors behind us and the pounding continued.

The doors to the operations room were reinforced, as was the bedroom doors upstairs, but that still didn't stop them trying to get in.

The banging and the shouting continued as the door vibrated.

Then the noise of a motor fired up, and the screaming, screeching sound began.

"They're cutting." We cocked our guns once more.

The sound of metal on metal was a lot louder than when we were outside, and it produced a thin whisp of smoke that rose up from the door crack. The noise stopped and was replaced by the sound of the motor idling, then cutting out.

"Now what?" Gina had her gun aimed squarely at the door.

Next was a chink, chink, chink sound of metal being struck, as what I could only imagine was a hammer and chisel on the other side of the door.

Then the sounds stopped.

Silence fell outside the door.

We waited.

We waited for a full minute.

Then we checked our watches, and waited a minute more.

Gina, Li and myself moved slowly towards the door and put our ears to the crack. Nothing.

We waited again.

All I could hear was the wind rushing in, playing a high note as it was funnelled down the corridor.

I looked at Gina. She put her hand on the doorknob and gently turned it.

I held my gun high as the door creaked open. She nodded and pulled as Myself, Li and two other agents swung our pistols into the opening and faced the corridor.

Empty.

We moved in silence back down towards the broken window, to see the back of the mob heading back down the lawn and out of sight.

"What...?" I was dumbfounded. My fellow agents were looking equally perplexed.

"Snipers? What do you see?"

"They are retreating back, ma'am. Some drones are still circling. Some have followed the hostiles back."

We lowered our weapons and headed back to the operations room. Des was still at his terminal. He had his arms folded round his chest and a smirk on his face.

"Analyst. Report."

"Check your phone, Doctor Hill."

I hadn't noticed that my phone had buzzed in my pocket. Adrenaline does that to you, I guess.

I took it out and saw a new message on the *EnkripChat* app.

The message has been sent to the Americans, time for bloodshed will come, now take your place at the font of the palace.

Li was in the doorway, and started clapping. "Brilliant. So, they're on their way back to the palace?

"Yup. Tipped of the Brits in Scotland Yard too." He slurped his coffee and leant back in his chair. "You're welcome, by the way."

"And what of Joel Thomas?" Li asked.

"He ditched his phone so we couldn't track him." She turned to Des. "Send out his description to British police."

"Yes, ma'am."

"And Li, Doctor Hill."

"Ma'am?"

"Get some rest. You look like crap."

Twenty-six

I have been staring at the ceiling for over twenty minutes now. It seems to be happening more and more recently that I wake up before the alarm goes off. This morning it was almost 7:35 a.m. when I rolled over and looked at the glowing red digits of my travel alarm clock, knowing it wouldn't start making its trademark bleeping sound until 8 a.m. precisely.

I'm not tired, I'm angry. No, frustrated. My logical brain tells me that the extra twenty-five minutes in bed probably won't make that much difference to my alertness, or my ability to function for the rest of day, but there is something inside me that just won't let me swing my legs from out under the duvet covers until that little gadget on the dressing table chirps into life and gives me permission.

And it also just feels good to be in bed.

I'm nervous now. I'm starting to wake up too much and think about the day ahead. Too much adrenaline is starting to flood my system. There's no hope of getting back to sleep now. I should just get up and get moving. Maybe get an early breakfast so I'm not rushing at the last minute.

Will things have changed?

Too nervous to eat. I know I should though. It would be better for me to eat a good meal to start the day than waste time trying to get back to sleep. An empty stomach would be far worse than slight fatigue later on in the day.

I wonder if anyone else is awake yet? Maybe I should take an early shower and go down to the restaurant and see who else is there.

7:38 a.m.

Come on, get up. I throw back the covers and get to my feet. I wander over to the coffee mate that I pre-loaded the night before and start it off. I shuffle over to the window and part the curtains.

London.

The street beyond the railings was empty. Normally on a weekday morning this would be a thoroughfare for commuters, teeming with traffic, but already the Secret Service is out in full force guarding the crash barriers that have been set up between Hyde Park and Park Lane in all directions as far as I can see from my window.

The coffee machine has finished brewing, so I go over and pour myself the first cup of the day. I am acutely aware that this is one of the last normal acts that I will do today, and probably one of the few cups of coffee I will get to drink until much later this afternoon.

As I get lost in my thoughts, I am brought back to reality by the phone ringing. It makes me jolt so much that I jerk my arm and my coffee goes everywhere. It's not boiling but hot enough that it scolds my leg.

"Shit," I hiss under my breath. I put the cup down on the table and wipe my hand on my t-shirt. My leg has gone bright red on my left thigh. It stings as I wipe the coffee off and walk over to my phone.

"Hey, you awake, Hill?" said a familiar voice.

"Yeah, have been for a while. Come on up."

I look down at my leg as a weird tingling sensation starts to build around my upper thigh. I can just sense the skin moving ever so slightly as the redness fades away.

There was a knock on my door.

"Come in."

I could hear the click of the heels before I saw her.

"Agent Hill."

"Agent Del Fonte."

"Gibson, you look awful."

"Thanks."

"No, I meant it. Are you OK?"

She was in another sharp suit, but her arm was in a sling. The wrist was bandaged but not in a cast, and she had a few scrapes and bruises to show for yesterday's efforts.

I looked out of the window for a moment, rain still pelting against the glass.

"Doctors from the hospital a few days ago said I am about to experience total organ failure, but the nano is the only thing keeping me going."

She sat on the chair next to me and put her hand on mine. "Gibson, I'm so…"

"Don't. I'm OK. I did what I need to do. I just want to enjoy the time I have. Find a nice house somewhere quiet. With a nice lawn."

"Lawn?"

"Long story."

We stood in silence and watched the world go by for a moment. I fantasied about what some of the people outside were doing. Some were probably off to work, some dropping kids to school, others just out to watch the motorcades go by.

Gina put a hand on my shoulder. "Come on Agent, time to face the music."

A put my jacket on and left the room with her. We had been called down to a debrief with our superiors, and it wasn't going to be pretty.

As we walked into the operations room, the noise stopped as everyone turned to stare at the pair of us.

There was silence for a moment as we locked eyes, the air seemed heavy with expectation.

One of the analysts stood and started clapping. As he did, others joined until the room was a riot of cheering and whooping. People came over to us and shook our hands, congratulating us on our achievement.

I felt like a hero.

Vice President Dawson was standing in the corner. "Hill, Del Fonte. In my office, please." A hush descended over the room.

"Well, it's been nice working with you all." I tried to make it come out as a joke, but instead it came out sounding more bitter.

We entered the room and Li was already there. We sat next to him. He smiled at as warmly, but at the same time was studying our faces, trying to assess our response.

Dawson was the first to speak. "First of all, are you both OK?"

Gina tapped her arm "Apart from this – but yes, we are... I am OK." She looked at me.

"Hill? How about you? Doctors tell me you are suffering? Is there anything I can do to help?"

"No. Thank you, sir. I'd just like some time, sir."

"Time?"

"Yes, sir. To take a break, sir, and recuperate."

The vice president sat back and opened a file in front of him. "Well, as far as I can see, you successfully killed of one of America's most wanted, and rooted out a mole within our own ranks. The press drones captured most of last night's activities with the hostiles – great move by the way, Del Fonte. In today's day an age of internet rumours, video evidence goes a long way to smooth things over with the public. The presidential approval ratings have shot through the roof."

I could hear the rumble of Marine One on its approach outside. "The official line is that it was a planned covert operation by the US, and McDonald had overseen the whole mission from day one."

Li sifted through the papers in the file. "Both of you are on three weeks gardening leave starting now and then desk duty for the foreseeable. You are lucky you are not being court marshalled."

"Yes sir. Thank you, sir." We both said in unison.

Marine One was overhead, and coming into view. "Time for us to go. You are both guests at the Buckingham Palace speech and will travel as civilians with the myself and first lady."

We stood and made our way out to the convoy. My heart beat went up a notch when I saw the Beasts. I was glad I was travelling as a civi. Don't think I'll ever be able to ride in the back of one of those again.

The president strode across the lawn but paused before getting in the car this time. He looked at myself and Gina, and saluted.

The convoy pulled away with McDonald on board, and moments later, the vice president and first lady came up to us as an armoured Mercedes pulled up alongside us.

She shook my hand. "Well done." A simple gesture, but she was a woman of few words.

SallyMac smiled at us as she and Dawson got in their car, and we got in the second and followed the convoy to Buckingham Palace.

***

Watching the president shake hands with the same supporters, and get groped by the same woman was surreal, but also strange to watch on the big screen. But hearing the *oohs* and *ahhs* of the crowd as they smiled along at McDonald's antics was heart-warming.

The people were craning their necks to get a better view as he moved up and down the rows and rows of crash barriers and broke out in laughter as the band struck up, giving him the hurry along as he played up to the camera.

That image again of him jogging fearlessly, with agents in their wrap around glasses, convoy of Cadillacs with the red and blue lights flashing on the front grills with the motorcycle outriders gave me goosebumps.

It had the same effect on the throng, too, as camera phones were held up, and hands were raised to touch smart glasses as just about everyone tried to capture the moment, with cries of 'Oh wow', and 'this guy is a real pro' rose up around.

I'm sure I caught Gina wipe away a tear as he bounded onto the stage in front of us, and shook hands with the King.

Now it was all eyes on the podium. My heart was in my mouth as the king's speech started. I knew that this time it would be different, but the sense of déjà vu was overwhelming.

The king delivered the same speech as before, and the crowd applauded as he stepped back and shook hands with the president.

Now it was McDonald's turn. After all this time, I could only guess at what he was about to say.

I had fought so hard for God only knows how many repetitions of the same day, just so that we could arrive at this moment, and hear this speech. Of course, I was nervous, but also excited, as I could sense the anticipation as McDonald cleared his throat.

"Thank you, Your Royal Highness. Before I begin, I would like to acknowledge the bravery of our American heroes, who, after a siege in a covert operation in a warehouse yesterday, and a brutal attack on our own house, including where my wife and children were staying, have successfully eliminated the terrorist known as Gim, and struck deep into the heart of his terrorist operation."

Cheers and applause rose up from the crowds.

"The selflessness, bravery and sense of national duty that drove these two patriots on has meant that we can all sleep safer at night, and showed the world that we will not be defeated by terrorists."

My pulse was quickening. Gina patted me on the shoulder.

"Whilst a few remain scattered, I am pleased to announce the fall of the so-called 'Hwarang', and the elimination of the terrorist threat to all global citizens of the world."

More cheers and applause rose up from the crowds.

"Thanks to our Secret Service agents Gina Del Fonte and Doctor Gibson Hill, you have not only helped to bring down a powerful terrorist organisation, but also gained intelligence that has made it possible for us to identify and stop a plan for a major terrorist attack in this very city today."

Gasps and murmurs came from all around us. I glanced over at the press pit, where reporters were on phones frantically trying to work out details of what he had just said.

"So, my heartfelt thanks go out to these two agents: Agent Hill, Agent Del Fonte, The world owes you a great debt."

The cameras swung over to us; our image projected on the big screens as we awkwardly waved.

McDonald waked across the stage to us, and gave me a big hug and slap on the back, and moved over and the same to Gina. He stepped back and saluted us, and we instinctively replied before he reapproached the podium.

He paused and looked out to the crowds. "But today marks a landmark in world politics. Not only are we celebrating a newly joined Korea, but a new path forward in peace for the nation.

"Today, in this NATO summit, we will be discussing the further way ahead, not only for the region of Korea, but for the rest of the world, as we harness our new found friendships, and work together to overcome global issues such as the climate, international healthcare and sustainable growth in labour, housing and food industries.

"But today marks more than that, as with the blessing of the senate and the house back home, and permission from the Royal household here in the United Kingdom, I will be setting out a new plan to bring about a new peace between our nations."

He paused, looking directly to camera.

"The US and the UK have recognised that escalation of armament has risen to the point of potential global annihilation. Some say that war is inevitable. That we are conditioned as human beings to fight. We are predisposed to attack each other for our freedoms, for our food, and for our wealth.

"But I say no. No to this old way of thinking. No to the violence. And no to the oppression.

"It takes a strong soldier to fight. But it takes an even stronger person to lay down their arms and talk."

Cheering erupted from the crowds.

"A strong leader must also lead by example. A strong and noble leader must show others the way. So, today, I am announcing that the US and the UK, alongside the other NATO countries, including Korea, will sign an agreement to begin a joint global taskforce of disarmament."

He paused again for effect.

"We will all, over the next five years, be decommissioning our weapons of global mass destruction, starting with our Zeus and Jupiter warhead programmes in the US, the Ascalon programme in the UK, and the Nuclear programmes in Korea."

The crowds cheered once more, all of the dignitaries on stage applauded the president.

"It is a sad fact, that our own warheads, and those of Korea, can reach each other's' countries in just thirty-two minutes, wiping out millions of people's lives in a matter of seconds, and plunging our precious planet into a nuclear winter for generations. This must stop right now!"

He pounded the podium as he said this last part.

"We will be signing the treaty after our lunch hosted by his royal highness, and forge a new era for all.

"So this day marks a turning point. A turning point for humanity. No longer will we hide behind our weapons. No longer will we have to use violence to be heard. No longer will our children suffer as a result of our petty differences. Today we stand up, as fellow human beings, and embrace our ability to talk, our ability to work together, and become the people we also wanted to be.

"Today, is the day we become one human race!"

He thumped the lectern with his fist to accent each word of the final sentence. Cheers erupted from the crowds in front. I was still scanning for threats, for pigs masks, and checking my phone app for any alerts. But all I saw was a sea of delight. Flags were waving, and fists were puncing the air. Some were even weeping with joy.

"Thank you to all of the NATO members for the support in this. God bless you all, and God bless America!"

He stood back and waved at the crowds, and turned to shake hands with the King once more as they all walked of the stage towards the palace.

As we too walked away, all of the dignitaries on stage filed out to meet their respective security details. Vice President Dawson walked alongside me.

He put an arm around my shoulder and smiled, as our image faded from the big screens above the palace. "You are to resign from the Secret Service with immediate effect, stating mental anguish and incapacity. You will be looked after, don't worry, I'll see to it you have a full pension, and a golden parachute so big your feet will never touch the ground."

He walked briskly away, and followed the president and first lady into the palace, as myself and Gina headed back to the cars.

Gina was in earshot of our encounter, and she sidled up beside me. "What was that all about?" Gina asked.

"I'm being kicked out of the Service, so it seems."

We got into the cars and pulled out of the rear of the stage and began the drive back to Winfield House. I was still turning over the strange conversation with Dawson in my head as the news feed came on our monitors. Unsurprisingly the announcement by McDonald was the major headline. The world apparently divided in opinion over the disarmament question.

The image showed us waving awkwardly to camera. Gina laughed. "We are not as media savvy as the president, are we?" I couldn't help but smile as I turned the sound up.

"…two agents who captured the terrorist and stopped a major incident in the capital. Sources are trying to confirm if it involved a bomb or weapon planted underneath the nuclear power station at Battersea."

We cut now to our correspondent in London, David Sheean. David…"

"Thanks, Nancy, yes President McDonald announcing radical disarmament of all NATO nations, in a treaty due to be signed later today in Downing Street, following a lunch at Buckingham Palace. You may recall that the president has faced tough criticism on his stance on Nuclear disarmament over the past fourteen months, including from the vice president and his own party. Sources say that…"

I turned the volume back down. I was watching London whisk by as we headed home, realising that this may be the last time I see her in a while, if ever. "Dawson fought in Korea, didn't he?"

Gina thought for a moment. "Yes, years ago though, before the unification. One of the first inside the old North Korea when they toppled Ji Young An. Made him a decorated hero."

"Wasn't he captured? Tortured first?"

"Yes, what became the Hwarang held him for three months. Say they nearly broke his mind. Tried to get him to defect."

"What were they called before the Hwarang?"

"Several things. Came from another group called the *Wonhwa*, or the *Original Flowers*, then the *Flowers of Korea*, then Gim came in with the group called the *Lynx*, then he overthrew the Flowers of Korea to form the Flowering Knights. Why do you ask?"

"So, the Lynx group was Gim's?"

"I believe so, yes."

"And they tortured Dawson?"

She had turned to face me now. "Where are you going with this?

I leant forward to our driver. "Turn the car around. Head back to the palace."

The driver looked in his rear-view mirror. "Sir? I am under orders to take you back to Winfield House."

"Just do it!"

"Why? What's happening?"

"What if Dawson was broken out there in Korea? He could be one of them. He could be the leak."

Gina was turning this over in her mind. "He certainly has all of the access to all of the intel. You think he will try something?"

"They sign the treaty after lunch."

The driver nodded and turned the car around.

***

I selected Li's name on my phone once again. I sat there and listened to a dial tone until it switched to voicemail. I ended the call without leaving a message. I dialled Salanski, and got the same result. My fingers were leaving sweat marks on the clean screen of my phone.

As we pulled up outside Buckingham Palace, the bulk of the crowds had dispersed, leaving the usual tourists hanging around taking pictures, with a few reporters milling around outside speaking to passers-by, trying to string out their program as long as they could.

Families and students were having their photos taken, or taking their own selfies with the palace behind them, and laughing as they battled the wind and rain; most of them posing and preening for the lens, blissfully unaware of the destruction that could have unfolded if things had panned out differently.

We exited the car and looked up at the building. I had never really stopped to admire it fully. It has a huge stone-looking facade; built like a fortress, and was surrounded by expansive iron gates that, today, were covered in police and private security.

Above us news helicopters were still circling, and I spotted the British copter that, in previous versions of today, had crashed and burned on the roof. I forced down a lump in my throat, and refocussed with a renewed sense of purpose at the task in hand.

We approached the first guard who put his hand absentmindedly on his gun holster as he saw us. We had been given security clearance to enter, but this was going to take some convincing.

We flashed our badges at the man, who was dressed in British military fatigues. He had a beret set at an angle and wore green and brown camouflage with heavy black boots.

Jeez, this kid looks barely out of nappies. I thought as we introduced ourselves.

"Agents Hill and Del Fonte, US Secret Service." We didn't even ask to gain entrance, as we walked past. *It's all about the attitude.*

We strode on, and found ourselves in the forecourt at the front of the palace; walking across that iconic reddish-brown expanse where tourists would flock to see the changing of the guards, and gawp at the men in red tunics and deerstalker hats as they stood for hours without moving.

They were there today; uniforms cleaned and shoes polished to within an inch of their lives. I'm sure I caught one of them give me a sideways glance as we walked past. *Gotcha.*

We headed to the great arch at the thrust of the building as more senior army officials saluted as we flashed our badges and hit the interior forecourt.

"So far, so good," Gina whispered to me as I marvelled at the grand palace now enveloping us.

A door to our right had opened, and five guys in suits were marching straight for us. The white curly earpiece cables marked them out as service, or private security.

By his walk that was half a pace ahead of the others, I could see the guy in the middle was in charge.

He was extending his hand has he approached. A good sign at least.

"Agent Matthews. British Secret Service." We shook as the other four just stared at us.

"Agents Hill, Del Fonte. What do we owe the honour?"

"We need to speak with Vice President Dawson and President McDonald on urgent security business." I tried to sound as confident as I could, knowing the code that was shared amongst senior security details.

Matthews waved his hands and took off his shades. "Listen, guys – great job by the way over at the docks. I heard what happened – takes some balls to take down Gim like that. I'm a fan, seriously." Here comes the sucker punch. "But you know I can't let you in. You were taken off the official invite list this morning. You know I'd love to help; but my hands are tied." He sighed and looked at the floor. "Look, I can get a message in, or why don't you just send a comm into your guys – must be a chain of command you can go through, right? Like I said, my hands are tied."

Gina was becoming stiffer in her posture. "Listen, Matthews, we are on urgent US Secret Service business, either you let us in, or—"

"Ma'am, I understand your position, I really do, but you are on British Royal Family property. I am the head of security here – and I just can't let you in."

I turned my back to Matthews to address Gina. I spoke quietly as if in confidence, but loudly enough so I could be overheard. "Gyo u i sin. They do not understand."

"Thank you, Agent Matthews, but we will have to report this to our superiors."

"Wait."

"Excuse me?" Matthews had moved closer to me so only I could hear. "What did you say?"

I waited a beat. "I am on a complex mission. Many moving parts are in play. Now is not the time or the place. I understand sa gun i chung, but I must also sal saeng yu taek."

Matthews put his shades back on, stood aside and said "Agents, please escort these comrades to the reception of NATO."

The other agents looked at each other, stood aside, and motioned for us to enter the palace.

Twenty-seven

The inside of Buckingham Palace was even more awe-inspiring than the outside.

Matthews and the other agents led us through the grand entrance and onto the deep red carpets of a wide square space.

The space itself was larger than the footprint of my apartment back in D.C., and had ceilings that were about three times the height.

Steps on each side led away from under white marble and gold walls, with sculptures set into each corner, watching our every move.

The grand entrance (as it was officially known) was quite dark; deliberately so, as we turned to the left and walked up the grand staircase (as that was also officially known), as the great expansive windows let the light pour in to give the impression of walking up into the light, allowing the colours to stand out and show off the grandness of the palace in its full glory.

Except it would if it wasn't raining quite so hard outside. Even as we moved deeper within the Palace, the wind was rattling at the windows, reminding us it was still there. Still not finished with us. Still wanting to be heard.

At the top of the grand staircase we were met by a man who was dressed in possibly one of the most expensive suits I had ever seen. He had the air of privilege about him, but still managed to give off a disarming air set to relax nervous and intimated guests. He introduced himself as the Assistant to the Master for Operations.

"Welcome, agents, it is our honour to host you at the palace. Please, follow myself and the footman, and will show you the way to the Ballroom."

We were led down one of the most impressive corridors I have ever walked down. Tapestries of former kings and queens lined the walls. There were grand chandeliers every thirty yards suspended from a ceiling that must have been two stories tall. Works of art were displayed in cabinets which included clothing, coats of arms, swords, axes, shields and official items from a bygone era.

"Gotta get me a palace one day," whispered Gina as her head swivelled all around as we walked.

I could hear the hubbub of the banquet reception as we entered the Ballroom. In the centre was a table one hundred and fifty feet long, and laid for dinner with fine china, flowers, and even a small light to illuminate each of the diner's plates.

But it was the odd details that impressed me. The carpets felt so luxurious and soft under foot, it was though I were walking in a pillow of foam as I walked.

All of the dignitaries were there, along with swarms of their own protection details.

Li came over to us as soon as we walked in. "What are you guys doing here? You were under orders to return to Winfield House."

"Sir, we believe we have found the mole, and the ringleader of the London terrorist operations, and felt it necessary to inform you immediately."

"And you never heard of a phone?"

"Sir, we tried to make contact but were unable."

Li pulled out his phone and tapped the screen. He furrowed his brow. "Huh." He turned to find one of the others. "Salanski, do you have any signal? My phone is dead."

Salanski punched his screen with his finger and held it up above his head. "Hmm."

Li checked over his shoulder and stepped closer to me, lowering his voice. "Hill, what do you know? Is there another threat?"

"Yes, sir, we believe that the insider…"

A slap landed on my shoulder. "Hill, Del Fonte. You should be recuperating."

My heart sank as I turned around. "Yes, Mr Vice President, sir. But we…"

"Sir, Agents Hill and Del Fonte believe they have found the mole in our ranks, and also have uncovered a comm—"

Dawson held up a hand. "Now, let's not make a scene in the palace in front of their Royal Highnesses; why don't we step outside and you can debrief these two agents. Li, please escort these two to Winfield House where you can talk."

Li held out his hands to beckon us outside. I kept my feet planted.

"Agent Hill?"

"Sir, it is of urgent national security reasons that I speak with the president immediately."

"Just not possible right now, he is over there talking to the French and German ambassadors, and then will be the guest of honour of the King at lunch. Not possible."

We were interrupted by a familiar female voice. "Agent Hill, Agent Del Fonte, what a lovely surprise." SallyMac had spotted us across the Ballroom and came over.

"Ma'am."

"Are you joining us this afternoon?"

"Agents Hill and Del Fonte were just—"

"Ma'am, we would be honoured."

"Please, come and say hello."

"Ma'am, I must insist that the agents return…"

"Oh, nonsense, Davis, they can say a quick hello now they are here." She hooked her arm around mine and we walked into the middle of the ballroom.

She smiled as we walked past the Spanish ambassador, and when we were out of earshot, she kept her smile, and spoke out of the corner of her mouth. "Now tell me what you are really doing here." She spoke quietly as we moved through the room.

I loved SallyMac, as most of the country did. She had that poise that you expect from a first lady, but also showed a shrewdness in politics. Whilst her husband was meeting world leaders, and making those grand podium speeches, she would often be found visiting a hospice, or talking to groups of children. The face of the people; charity work at the forefront of her agenda. The perfect spouse for the commander-in-chief.

People would often tell her things that they could not tell the president; she often was the one who ended up being a key figure in peace negotiations, due to her humility and humanity, and an ability she had to get people to confide in her.

I glanced at her as we passed dignitaries and footmen moving past us.

"Ma'am. I believe there is a mole inside our ranks orchestrating terrorist activities."

I caught her eye, not wanting to say the name out loud, knowing the close relationships that the top people have in the White House. I needn't have worried; she was one step ahead of me.

"David Dawson has been... off ever since we arrived. And he seemed keen to get rid of you. Ah, my husband."

McDonald was talking to a group of people as we approached, and when he saw me his face lit.

"Ah, please, ambassadors, meet Secret Service agent, Doctor Gibson Hill. The man who helped engineer our mission to bring down the Hwarang yesterday. Agent Hill, the foreign ambassadors of Germany and France, gentlemen, this is Agent Hill."

Handshakes and more backslapping went around the group.

"Sir, I need to show you something of upmost importance," I said as I pulled out my phone.

McDonald looked at the screen for a moment, but kept his face straight. He read the screen twice more looked back at me as he handed the phone back over. I tapped a button and put the handset away.

The president slowly scanned the room around him as a Secret Service agent from Ukraine glanced at his smart watch; and then moved through the room.

We followed him as he moved past us, and along the dining table towards Dawson.

He subtilty moved into position next to the vice president.

The agent from Ukraine was speaking to Dawson. Dawson spoke back. I could not hear what he was saying, but he was jabbing his finger at the chest of the Ukrainian agent.

Then the agent grabbed Dawson's wrist. He started shouting as Li and Salanski moved in at speed.

The room had fallen into a stunned hush as Li and Salanski wrestled the man to the floor.

"Hands where I can see them."

The Ukrainian agent was on the floor but fighting. "His watch. His watch has a poison."

McDonald had moved towards them. I followed to listen in.

"Li, Salanski, get this man out of here. Where is the ambassador for Ukraine?"

"Just check his watch – his watch is a weapon."

"Dawson? What is he saying?"

"Clearly out of his mind, Joyce. Take him away, guys."

"Show me your watch."

"Come on, Joyce, you don't need to make a scene."

"That is an order, Vice President. Hand over your wristwatch."

"Sir, I'm sure it's just…"

"Watch. Now."

He took off his watch and Li took it from him. "Sir, I think I should. Just in case."

"Go ahead, Agent Li."

All eyes in the room were on us as Li turned the watch over in his hands. He tapped the glass and flipped it over, pushing and pulling the strap and face as he studied the timepiece.

He looked back at McDonald. "Seems clean, sir."

"OK, can we get this guy out of here now?" Dawson was red in the face and waved his hand at the man still being pinned down by Salanski. "And give me that back."

"Sir." Li held out the watch to Dawson, but as he was about to take it when the agent gave a kick that Salanksi reacted to by arching his back, and regripping the agent's arms. Li glanced down as this happened, and took his eye off of Dawson's hand, just as he was about to take the watch.

The watched slipped from his grip and tumbled down. Turning over and over in the air as it fell. It hit Dawson's shoe and bounced back up with a *click*.

The pin had shot out of the side to reveal a small, clear vial of pale blue liquid.

The vial bounced twice, span and came to a rest at McDonald's feet. It glistened in the lights of the ballroom, its blue sheen speaking out in the chaos. *Guilty* it whispered as Dawson's mouth snapped shut.

"Clear the room!" Li ordered everyone out. All of the dignitaries were dragged out by their protection, and we moved in on Dawson who was turning to flee.

"Vice President Dawson, you are under arrest under the Counter-Terrorist Act, you…" I began to talk but Dawson was fast. He dropped to the floor, hand reaching out for the vial. He grabbed it in a fist and slammed it into his mouth. The sound of crunching glass came from his jaws as blood and blue liquid oozed down his chin. Before any of us could react, he swallowed it – blood, glass and all – and looked up at the circle around him. He started laughing, a maniacal, diseased laugh of a condemned man.

Blood oozed from his gums as he began to foam at the mouth.

Twenty-eight

Outside I sat on the edge of a small wall in the courtyard of the palace.

I should have been admiring the building I was in, taking in the architecture, soaking up the atmosphere. But I wasn't. I was beat. I just wanted to close my eyes and let the rain wash away my sins. Let it cleanse me and make me feel whole.

I was shaking from the comedown of the adrenaline, and the cold outside. But I didn't care. It felt good just to sit still. I could sit here for hours, days, even.

I knew that I couldn't, but in these magic moments, it felt like time didn't pass, and all of the world had stopped around me.

Gina broke the spell.

"Hey," she said as she sat beside me.

"Hey," was all I could manage back at her.

Li and Salanski had come over to join us. Li was the first to speak of the pair. "All VIPs are safe. McDonald is headed back to Winfield House. We should go to. For a debrief."

He handed me a cup. I didn't even ask what was in it, just downed the hot steaming liquid and felt grateful.

I studied the floor of the courtyard. The rain bounced up off the ground like a dance that would never cease. Rivers of water now flowed away into the storm drains that were struggling to deal with the volume.

I took a deep breath before I spoke. "I resign."

Li took off his shades and twisted them in his hands. "Denied. You're not thinking clearly. You have just been through a traumatic experience. Wait a few days then we can talk."

I finished my coffee. "No. I have had enough time to think. I have seen enough now. I want out. I'll do the debrief and give you all the information I have, then I want my pension and my cheap gold watch."

Li laughed at this. He slapped me on the knee. "You are a credit to your country, Doc."

A rumble of thunder reverberated around us. The lightning illuminated the courtyard.

"What happened to Thomas? Did we find him?" Salanski was lying back, allowing the rain to wash him, too.

"We'll catch up with him soon. He'll make a mistake at some point."

"Do you think he was one of the ringleaders?"

"In part. Dawson was the main guy. Thomas was most likely the tech in control of all of the phone messages, and the hacks."

Salanksi let out a low whistle. He too had a coffee, but was using to keep his hands warm.

"Where do you think he went? There must be other guys working with him? Also has to be close by, right? To tap into phones like that you have to be able to see them, right?" Salanski was sitting upright now. I could see his mind spinning, wanting nothing more to catch the traitors to his country.

"There will be a safe house. I location they all head back to if things go wrong." Li was joining in the brainstorming session. "But... could be anywhere." He looked around the courtyard. "London is a big city."

The palace was protecting us from the winds, but making a low whistling sound as it forced its way through the archways and columns. Like it was playing a note for the audience it held captive.

"Shit." I stood up. The adrenaline coming back into my bloodstream.

All eyes had turned to me.

"What? What is it?"

I looked at Gina. "The gunman. The gunman on stage."

Gina raised an eyebrow. "There was no gunman?"

"Yes, I know; in a different version of today. He shot McDonald and then ran. Well, I mean, tried to shoot him."

I waved my hands away at the thought. "Never mind. Point is, I chased him once around the corner from here. Down an alleyway. He bolted into a doorway. I thought it was just random at the time, But—"

"Woah, wait," said Li. "What do you mean McDonald was shot at? When did this happen?"

"Long story. I'll explain later. But it's just a hunch."

***

The four of us entered the alleyway with guns drawn. Li had given me his spare, and I was leading the group to the doorway I had seen the Korean agent disappear into, in what seemed like an age ago.

We reached the doorway I knew to be open, with Salanski behind me, and Gina and Li flanking the opposite side, I reached out a hand and turned the knob.

It opened, as I knew it would, and Li swept in, gun drawn.

Once we were all in, we were faced with a staircase in front of us. This door obviously led straight up to a flat on the first floor. We ascended the staircase and reached another door at the top.

I reached out for the handle, which again, turned in my grip.

The door was old, and, just like an old movie, creaked as it opened. We all filed in, guns again drawn in a flanking formation.

The scene we were faced with stunned me.

Twenty-nine

We were in what could be best described as a student bedsit. A teenager was sitting at a desk in front of a large bank of computer monitors, each showing something different.

Several of them were showing news feeds, but, as I looked closely, realised that it was all from the same location, just at a different angle.

They were all from an elevated position in front of Buckingham Palace.

The rest of the screens looked like a conference call was happening. Lots of other teens and young adults were on screen, all wearing headsets just like our guy at the desk, but some weren't. Some were generals, or at least high-ranking military from different backgrounds. I recognised the Korean uniform on one man straight away, and a couple of Europeans on other screens; the others, I could not place.

Later I would try and tot up the people. There would have to have been at least thirty civilians, and fifteen military, with another ten or so people in suits on this mass conference call.

I took a good lingering look at the images in front of me.

There was also a guy in the shadows in the corner of the room, facing us as we came in. It was Joel Thomas.

He leapt up when he saw us. "What are you doing here?" His eyes were wide, and he was holding a mobile phone.

The kid on the desk span around to face us, and as soon as he registered that we were holing guns, put his hands in the air. They were shaking. "Please. Please don't shoot. I'm only doing this for the money."

"Both of you, hands above your head, and lay face down on the floor."

The faces on the screen all started noticing what was going on, and, one by one, all started exiting the call.

"What is this?" asked Salanski. "Who are those people?"

Joel started laughing as he lay on the floor in front of us. "You don't get it, do you?"

"Enlighten me."

"Those people," he said, glancing up the screens, "are just the tip of the iceberg."

Li cocked his gun. The kid whimpered.

"Those were military and political leaders from across the globe."

"You're lying."

He chuckled to himself once more. "You guys. You guys make me laugh. You think you know what's really going on? Do you think you have a handle on these things? You are just like everybody else. All of those people out there, in front of Buckingham Palace, all of those people out on the streets. All go about their daily lives blissfully unaware of who is really in control."

Li stepped forward and presses his gun to Joel's temple. "Explain."

Joel sighed. "Do you think it's the politicians that are really in control? Of course not. The real power lies in the money. Or rather, the individuals and families and companies that control the banks. It's the people that sign multinational defence contracts, it's the people behind the scenes that wield the real power. Politicians – they are just puppets." He paused and turned his head towards the screens.

"Those people up there are military leaders, bankers and defence contractors. Powerful people, way over and above government. Economic crashes? It's them that profit. War? Same again. Global disasters? Bingo.

"You see, terrorism is just a state sponsored thing. You think Gim was the mastermind? Na, he's just another puppet. Has lunch with us at noon and then goes on camera to tell the world he hates us. All part of the global system of control.

"Control for the ants like you. Ants they look down on and squash when they feel like it. Pawns they can control through social networks, the mainstream media and advertising."

He pointed up at the left of the screens. "You see those feeds of Buckingham Palace? All of the global media's feeds of today. We own most of them now. We tell them what to say, and when to say it.

"Now McDonald. He's good. And his wife, too. They are trying to root us out from the inside. But they underestimate the power we have. The power of the media, the power of suggestion. You see, one correctly placed news story can alter public perception just like that. It's funny."

"Why is it so funny?"

He turned back to Li. "Funny how most people don't even realise that a small handful of hidden faces control the world."

Now it was my time to laugh. I started chuckling, my shoulders heaving up and down. I looked over at Salanski, who started laughing too. Soon, all four of us were sharing the joke.

Joel looked puzzled. "What? What is so funny?"

"You see," I began. "The media can put out a story, spin it all around, upside down, you know – the full works. But I can spin a story, too."

Joel cocked his head at me.

"You see, the media has a lot of control, granted. But the people have power now, too."

"What are you going on about?"

I paused for effect. "Look at the crowds out there, Joel, and tell me what they are al doing?"

He twisted and looked at the news feeds. "I don't know what you mean."

"You see, the truth is, that they are witnesses to history. They see and hear things and tell each other."

"Oh, come on, opinion only goes so far."

I laughed once more. "Oh, Joel, all this tech and you can't see it."

"See what?"

"How news is really shared these days. How it is not the news outlets who have all the power, or the bankers, or who holds the money."

I touched the sides of my shades, and issued a command. "Stop streaming."

"What?" Joel was getting to his feet.

"Down on the ground." Li and Salanski pointed their guns at his head.

"I Just uploaded that, and all those faces to my social media accounts. And by the way – I have quite a following, after today – haven't you heard?"

Li and Salanski both chuckled. "This man is a star."

I turned back to the floor. "Joel Thomas. You are under arrest."

Thirty

"…said the White House in a statement that Vice President Dawson was struck down with a sudden illness, and our sources say that he was rushed to hospital after falling ill during the lunch hosted by the king and Royal family at Buckingham Palace, but died after in hospital. In other news, it is claimed by the US that the terrorist group known as the Hwarang has been brought down after a daring assassination in London of the group's leader, the man known simply as 'Gim'. White House officials refuse to comment as to the speculation of a mole inside the White House that orchestrated the attempted terrorist attack and attempted hack of London's infrastructure during the NATO summit. Our correspondent in Washington…"

Gina turned off the TV. "All spin," she muttered as I turned off the radio.

The car hummed along quietly as the English countryside flew past us. We were in a new hire car, and it was so quiet inside the cabin, if I closed my eyes, I could have fallen asleep forever.

But I wanted to savour every moment that I could. The weather was still atrocious, but I didn't care. I loved the rain. It made me feel like a kid who was excited by the storms when I used to watch them from my classroom window.

I squeezed my body down into the seat and fiddled with the radio once more. I wanted music this time, not the boring dirge of the news.

I found a station that played oldies, so I cranked the volume and sat back.

Gina's fingers tapped on the steering wheel as the old church spire came into view.

We crested the familiar hill and appeared in front of the old barn. Gina had called ahead, and so Hart was less shocked when we arrived (His gun was pointing at the floor this time).

"David Hart," he said as he offered his hand to me.

"I know," I said as I took it.

We exchanged a few pleasantries for a while and then went into the barn where Hart strapped my arms down to the gurney.

"You could have replacement nano still," he said as he prepped his computer.

"To risky," I said. "If anyone finds out what it can do…"

"I hear ya, buddy." He came over to the bed. "But you realise the consequences?"

The rain was subsiding outside. The storm had been raging for about a week now, and it showed signs of breaking. And I think I knew why.

"You got word back to the old lab of Doctor Craven?"

"Yup. All about to be destroyed. Including all his notes. No one will ever have this technology."

"How long will I have?" I asked, not really wanting to know the answer.

Hart busied himself at his terminal once more, not wanting to look me in the eye. "Before you start deteriorating? Could be a month, could be more, could be less." He sighed as he finished his setup. "I'm sorry, Gibson. I wish it was better news."

Gina came over and held me hand. "Please reconsider." Her eyes were red, and she looked like she hadn't slept in days.

"Honestly. I'm happy. Once I die, I reset time. And we saved tens of thousands of lives over the last few days. That, I can live with."

Hart looked gravely at his screen. "Once I remove it, there is no going back."

I closed my eyes and nodded. Hart punched buttons on his keyboard as syringes moved into place.

I looked down at my body. I was dressed in a pair of jeans and a sweater. A far departure from the Secret Service suit I had gotten used to over the years.

It's funny how some things feel familiar. The smell of this barn would be something I would remember until my last days, and somehow, look back on this time fondly, as if nostalgically thinking back on a more dynamic time of my life.

I had already planned my retirement. Knew what my place was going to look like. I knew exactly what my flowerbeds would contain, and how neat I wanted my lawn to be. I had even suggested that Gina come and help me do it all; a notion she had initially refused, but had been talked around to soon after she, like me, had quit the service.

Hart tapped the screen and looked back at me. "It's done."

I thanked him and said I wanted to be alone for a moment, as I walked outside and deeper into the trees behind his house.

The path I was following led me down to a stream where the water burbled over rocks, and followed me out to a clearing.

I carried on walking up the hill for a few minutes, until I reached the top and had a view right out to the coast.

Between me and the ocean were a few small towns, trees and roads that all found their way down to the beach. It didn't look far, so I set out on a slow stroll to find out what was there.

The rain had stopped, and the winds had died down to a gentle breeze.

The grass under foot reminded me of the carpets back in Buckingham Palace, and the air smelt of salt and sea.

I felt a sense of calm that I had never felt before as that clouds parted, and the sun came out overhead.

Today was going to be a sunny day after all.

THE END

CPSIA information can be obtained
at www.ICGtesting.com
Printed in the USA
BVHW032046050421
604235BV00001B/93